Music and Misadventure

Modern Magick, 6

Charlotte E. English

1

'So,' said Jay. 'Tell me again. What exactly are we doing here?'

Here was a breezy, grassy plain adorned by craggy chunks of rock nicely arranged in a ring. Two rings, actually, one inside the other; swaying gently in the centre of both was me.

'Visiting my mother,' I said, swallowing nausea. I thought I was getting used to flying down the Winds of the Ways, but today...

'Ves,' said Jay, wearily. 'Visiting one's mother consists of popping by for tea and scones on a Saturday afternoon, and having a cosy chat. It does *not* consist of flying off to the other side of the country at a moment's notice, with nothing but a set of co-ordinates to inform us as to her precise location, and after six years of total silence on both sides.'

'All right,' I said, venturing a step or two beyond the confines of the inner circle. 'We are riding nobly to my mother's side to afford her whatever assistance lies within our power.'

'Six years, Ves.'

'I heard you.'

'There was a question in there.'

'Got it.'

'Actually, there were several.'

I had no answers for Jay, certainly none that would satisfy him, so I said nothing. He had brought us to a henge in Birkrigg, Cumbria, otherwise known as Druid's Temple, and it proved, to my satisfaction, to be located very near the sea. I filled my lungs with fresh ocean air, turned my face (probably tinged with green) to the brisk wind, and indulged in a moment's reflection.

I need you to come here at once, Mother had said, having called me out of the blue. *And bring those pipes of yours.* She had not, of course, said why. Nor had I been able to prise an answer from Milady, as to why she had obligingly given my personal phone number to my mother.

Mother dearest had also insisted upon Jay, equally without explanation. A few minutes after she had hung up on me, a text had arrived, containing nothing but a string of numbers: map co-ordinates.

They'd led us, so far, to the Cumbrian coast.

None of it made any sense.

'If your mother asked for your help,' I said, without turning around. 'Wouldn't you go running?'

'Yep,' said Jay. 'But that's—'

He stopped, but I had a feeling he'd been planning to say, *but that's different.* Maybe it was. He had, by all appearances, a close relationship with his family.

Privately, I couldn't fault him for a degree of indignation. Upon finding myself so peremptorily summoned across the country without so much as a *Hi, daughter, how are you?* I'd had to swallow a flicker of pure rage. How could she dare to—

No, no thinking like that. At least it was communication, after so much silence. At least she wanted me for *something.*

And then there was the fact of Milady's interference. Was she just being neighbourly, and trying to put me on better terms with my family? Or did she know something about my mother's purpose that I didn't?

Curse my insatiable curiosity, I had to find out.

'She's my mother,' was all I could find to say to Jay, which had to be explanation enough. After all, I only had the one.

Jay accepted this with a nod, though the frown did not clear from his brow. 'Okay,' he said. 'So. Sheep Island.'

Mother's co-ordinates proposed to land us in the middle of a tiny spit of land only fifteen acres across, populated with (despite the name) nothing but grass, and with (as far as we could find out) nothing whatsoever to recommend it to anybody's notice. It had taken us some little time to plot a route. Waymastery to Druid's Temple; take to the skies, and straight on to Sheep Island, taking great care not to fall into the sea en route.

I summoned Adeline.

'Do you know how to ride?' I said to Jay, as I tucked my silver pipes back into their snug hiding nook.

'We've had this conversation before. Answer's still no.' Jay shaded his eyes against the mid-morning sun as he watched Addie's pale form descend from the skies. Her broad, beautiful wings sent gusts of air washing over both of us as she spiralled down and landed a few feet away, shaking her head with a whinny. Then he looked sideways at me. 'Why do you ask? I've flown Air Unicorn a few times. Still breathing.'

I took a moment to croon endearments into Addie's ears before replying. I also fed her from the bag of fresh, still-warm chips I had in my pocket. We'd stopped off at a chippie before sailing away on the Winds, and I'd managed to resist the temptation to eat more than a few of them. I felt proud. 'This time, we aren't flying. Or, not yet.'

'What? Why not?'

'For one thing, it's very windy up there. Did you see the way Addie was buffeted around on the descent?' I swung myself up onto Addie's broad back and took hold of the silvery rope she wore for my (I think) benefit.

'We've flown on windy days before.' Jay eyed Adeline uneasily.

I smiled brightly down upon him. 'For another thing, it's a beautiful day for a ride. Come on.' I patted Addie's back, the bit right behind myself.

'Nope.' Jay stepped back, shaking his head.

'Come on! You won't die.'

'People have died this way before.'

'People have died in cars before, and you still drive. Hup.'

Jay just stood there with a frozen look.

'You know,' I said conversationally, stroking Addie's neck. 'I heard a rumour from Home. Apparently *some-body's* got a very nice, very shiny motorbike.'

'And?' Jay folded his arms, and did not budge a single inch.

I rolled my eyes. 'If you'll drive and ride a motorbike, what's wrong with a horse?'

'Unicorn.'

'Right.'

Jay looked away. 'I fell off a horse when I was eight. Broke some bones. I was lucky to be alive, so said the doc.'

'Ah...' I pictured a younger, smaller Jay, snapped like a bundle of twigs, and shuddered inwardly.

'It was my first riding lesson.'

'And you haven't ridden horseback since.'

'Only Air Unicorn, which was bloody terrifying, so thanks for that. But nobody died, and it's... not quite the same. There's no traffic up there, no cars — nothing that's going to come roaring up behind your placid unicorn, blaring its horn and scaring the creature into bolting off with you.'

I nodded slowly, and surveyed the surrounding countryside. Green. Deserted. 'If we take a gentle run down the coast, keep away from the roads?'

'Can't we walk? I don't mind walking.'

'Try it for two minutes. Come on.' I beamed encouragingly.

Jay approached, with the caution of a man preparing to diffuse a bomb. He laid one hand warily upon Addie's back.

Addie nudged him with her velvety nose.

'That's a hi,' I interpreted.

'Hi, death trap,' said Jay, but he gently patted her back, and received only a derisive snort by way of reply.

Jay took a deep breath. 'Right, then.'

Three minutes later, Jay was up behind me with a death grip around my waist, and we were ambling along at a peaceful, and deadly dull, walk. 'You okay back there?' I called.

'Fine,' he said through gritted teeth, and I pretended not to notice that he was shaking.

'You sure? Totally fine?'

'Yep.'

'Okay! We're going to canter.'

'What's a canter— *argh*,' Jay said, as Addie sped up to a smooth, rolling pace just shy of a full-blown gallop. His arms tightened around my waist, but that was okay, I could manage without air if Jay could manage without sanity.

'Isn't this great!' I shouted, lifting my face to the wind. I imagine I was grinning like an idiot. I do so *love* a ride along the cliffs, all that sea just over the way, shining in the sun and smelling amazing...

Jay said something. I thought it was *I hate you,* but considering that my hair (current colour: amber) was streaming back into his face and he'd apparently received a mouthful of it, it was hard to be sure.

Luckily for me, considering I'd cleverly disabled my navigator, Addie needed little direction. We cantered joyously (well, two of us did) all the way south down the Cumbria coast, and when we ran out of land Adeline beat her beautiful wings and up we soared. Vibrant green land and sparkling sea fell away beneath us. Jay, poor Jay who I'd soullessly abused, gave a great sigh and sagged against me like a sack of cement. 'I hate you,' he said, and there was no doubt about it this time.

'I know, but I forgive you.'

Jay snorted into my shoulder.

The flight was but a short one, to my regret. I wanted to stay longer in the air. Was it only because I so much enjoyed the flying, or was I moved to procrastinate against whatever lay ahead? That lump of concrete swelling in my stomach was *not* dread. Not a bit of it.

Too late now. A speck of green materialised among the waves; Adeline swooped gracefully down; within moments we were deposited upon a grassy sward presumably answering to the name of Sheep Island. The moment we were both restored to our own two feet, Addie snatched the remains of the chip bag from my pocket and took off at a thundering gallop, aiming for the sea. To my infinite surprise, she neither took off at the water's edge nor ploughed into the water. She charged straight *over* the water, her silvery hoofs sending up clouds of sea-spray, and soon vanished into the distance.

'Did you know she could do that?' said Jay.

'Nope.' I looked him over carefully. 'For a man recently emerged from an ordeal of terror, you look good.'

Jay smoothed back his hair. His hands had almost stopped trembling. 'Flatterer.'

'I am shameless.' I took a look around, turning in a full circle. Nothing met my eye but grass, waving gently in the wind, and beyond that, the grey-blue water of the sea. 'Does it strike you that there's a distinct lack of mothers about?'

'Did we get the co-ordinates right?' Jay stared at his phone, and began to type.

I wandered off. Since my feet showed signs of wanting to trail feebly about with unbecoming reluctance, I made them adopt a fine, purposeful stride, and went off at a good clip.

Two minutes later, I found Mother.

'Jay?' I called, winded, and stared dazedly up at the suddenly-distant blue sky above me. My body protested its recent treatment at my uncaring hands — loudly — and I groaned. I lay flat, at least ten feet beneath the surface, with the craggy walls of dug-out ground rising around me. I'd fallen face-first into a pile of rocks.

'Ves?' Jay's voice was nowhere near distant enough.

'Watch out for the—' I yelled, and stopped. No point wasting breath on the rest.

'Crap,' wheezed Jay.

'Hi,' I said, with a big smile for my unhappy colleague.

Jay, recumbent and wincing about three inches away, just looked at me.

'Anything broken?'

Jay shook his head — more in disbelief than in answer to my question, I thought — and pushed himself up onto his elbows. 'This,' he said distinctly, 'is the worst mission ever and we've only just arrived.'

'Then it can only get better, can't it?' I dragged myself to my feet and conducted a quick survey of our landing site. Dirt. Packed earth; recently turned earth; little pegs stuck into the ground and looped around with strings, marking out a grid... aha. Archaeological dig site.

And along one side, farthest from the sea, an area of shadow. The ground there was dug deeper down — in fact, the wide mouth of a passage yawned there, its walls fitted with stone. It sloped, rapidly disappearing underground.

Its entrance was occupied.

'Hello, Mother,' I said, with a feeble smile and an awkward wave.

'Cordelia,' said she.

2

WHEN MY MOTHER SAID she'd given me the most beautiful name she could think of, it might be of interest to know that she was referring, more or less, to her own. Delia Vesper sat inside the mouth of the cave, propped against the dark rock wall, and shrouded in so much shadow that I could barely make out the details of her form.

'Is that your Waymaster?' said Delia from the darkness.

'Yes, but we tend to call him Jay.'

'Jay Patel,' said Jay. 'Hello, Mrs. Vesper.' He was so polite, I'm sure he would have shaken hands with her if he could.

Her voice, when it came again, was wry. 'It's Miss Vesper, but you may call me Delia.'

Further questions bloomed in Jay's mind, judging from the brief glance he made at me. I privately hoped I wouldn't have to answer too many of them.

It occurred to me that my mother hadn't moved, and that seemed rude, even for her. All right, then. If she wouldn't come out, I'd have to go in. 'So,' I said, and ducked into the mouth of the cave. 'Why are we here?' With a flick of my finger I summoned a tiny fireball, just enough to cast a light. It's about as much as I am capable of in the fireball arena.

My mother made a frightful sight. Her skin, always pale, was white as wax. Her shabby, old clothes and auburn hair were matted with dirt, the latter tangled, but these things were not so unusual for her.

The blood, however, was.

I fell to my knees beside her. 'Mother,' I said sharply. 'You're hurt.' She was cradling one arm, her breath coming short; it must have cost her some effort to speak in such measured tones.

'A bit.' She eyed me with the same old challenging look: would I, *dared* I, imply that she could not fully take care of herself?

The dried blood soaking her clothes — hell, my very presence on Sheep Island — proved that, this time, she could not. I wasn't having it. 'You should have told me,'

I hissed. 'I'd have brought Rob. You need medical attention.'

'I haven't died yet, have I?' She would have shrunk away from me, I think, if she had not been so hurt.

I may have growled. 'Mother,' I said firmly. 'Don't be so damned difficult. You know you need help, or you would not have called us in. So. Tell us what happened, and then we can decide what to do for you.'

Jay had joined us by this time. He hovered, as uncertain as I was as to what to do for my stubborn parent. He made some attempt at scrutiny, but with the dim light and his lack of medical knowledge, he was as powerless as I.

We sat, and waited.

Mother gave a short, harried sigh. 'I came here a month ago with a team. We'd heard tell of a village that once existed upon one of these islands. Thought to be decimated by plague somewhere in the 1300s, and fallen into ruins. My kind of thing.' She spared a brief smile.

In case you hadn't guessed, my mother's an archaeologist. She specialises in the unearthing of lost magickal settlements, and the medieval era's her speciality. I could well imagine that such a rumour would light her fire.

'Well, we started here. At first we thought ourselves mistaken. You no doubt saw as you came in that the terrain here is largely flat and undisturbed. Buried villages tend to leave some lumps and bumps here and there, where earth and grass have grown over chunks of toppled buildings—'

'We know that, mother,' I interrupted. I would not normally be so impatient, but for heaven's sake, the woman was bleeding. Judging from her face, she was lucky not to have bled to death.

'But,' she said, as though I had not spoken. 'Hank — you remember Hank? Reads every book ever written — Hank said that these islands had a strong gnome population around that era, and—' Here she paused for breath, growing a shade or two paler. '—he was right. The village was below. We found it after three weeks, and, well...' Unbelievably, she gave a tiny snort of laughter. 'It wasn't as deserted as we were hoping.'

'What did you find?' I prompted, when she fell silent. Surely, she did not mean that gnomes still lived down there. They weren't known for violence.

'Lindworm.'

Lindworms are a species of dragon, the wingless kind. Vicious. Cave-dwelling. Sometimes treasure-guarding, but sometimes just mean. 'Did anybody else make it out?'

Silently, mother shook her head.

I pushed thoughts of Hank from my mind — he'd been a sporadic but genial presence during my short childhood at home, and though I had never thought to see him again, the news of his death cost me a swift stab of pain.

But mother was bleeding.

'I've lost a hand,' she said suddenly.

'Shit. Mother, you — why didn't you call for help?'

'I did.'

'I don't mean me! You need an ambulance!'

'Cordelia.' Unbelievably, my mother ceased clutching her wounded arm and instead fastened her one remaining hand around my wrist. 'I couldn't. You don't know what else we found down there.'

'Was it worth this much secrecy? You could've died waiting for us to arrive! Gods, maybe you still could—'

'Stop *fussing*. If I was going to die I would have done it already. Listen. Look at this island. Does it not strike you that it is *far too small* to host a lindworm underneath?'

'Yes.'

'It is not there now.'

'What? How do you know?'

'Why do you think I am still alive? It vanished. *Vanished,* Cordelia. And I saw how. There's a gateway down there.'

'A gateway.'

'I don't know where it goes, but we need to find out.'

'*Need*? You've lost a bloody hand!'

Her jaw set, she stared at me, eyes glinting in the firelight. 'I've sacrificed a hand for this. Hank and Petra and Lily have died for this. We are *not leaving.*'

We glared at each other for a few, long moments, each simmering with fury.

Until Jay, softly, chuckled. 'Some aspects of Ves's personality are becoming clear,' he said to my mother. 'She's the most stubborn person I've ever met, and once she's got interested in something, there is no stopping her.'

She, to my surprise, gave a wry smile. 'That's my girl.'

Jay looked, enquiringly, at me, and I understood that it was my job to decide.

Damn it.

'Answer me one thing,' I said to my mother.

'Anything.'

Interesting carte blanche, and unusual; no time to take advantage of it. 'Why did you call me in? Haven't you got hosts of other, highly qualified archaeologist acquaintances you could have called for help?'

'I don't need an archaeologist. Weren't you listening? They were eaten alive. So was I.'

'Right, but—'

'This isn't about archaeology anymore. I needed an adventurer, and who better than you?'

'What do you *mean*, who better than me? You haven't appeared to remember my existence for *six years!* Presumably, anyone's better than me!'

'We can talk about that,' said my mother.

'While you're quietly bleeding to death? I think not.'

'I'm not bleeding to death. Barely bleeding at all, anymore.'

'How did you manage that?'

'Fire magick. Cauterised it.'

I blanched. Shit, my mother was brutal. 'Fine. Okay, you're not about to die. But you don't look good, mother, permit me to say. You still need medical help, and a lot of rest.'

'Sure,' said mother. 'Later. First we find out where that gate goes.'

'Why are you so interested?'

'We're in Cumbria. In case you weren't aware, it's riddled with folklore.'

'The juicy kind. I know. But most of those kinds of stories are rubbish, mother. You know that. Fairy stories for non-magickers.'

'Most. Not all.'

'You've got some particular tale in mind, haven't you?'

'Might do. We can talk about that, too — later.'

I sighed. Jay was right: my mother and I were fairly equally matched, but I knew when I was losing. 'I still wish you'd told me what was going on. I would *definitely* have brought Rob.' I briefly considered sending for him, but by the time he got here... for all my mother's claims, I still wasn't at all sure she was out of danger.

Best to get it over with.

That said... lindworms were no picnic.

'We're going to need one hell of a plan,' I said.

'Actually,' said my mother, 'I was hoping those pipes of yours would do the trick.'

'I've never tested them on a lindworm before,' I said cautiously.

'But their effectiveness is renowned. Legendary. How *did* you get hold of them?'

'We can talk about that. Later.'

She sighed. 'I deserved that.'

I thought about it. I may not have tested them on a lindworm, but I had tested them on griffins very recently — twice. And we were still here. 'We can try it,' I said. 'But you're staying up here, at least until we are sure it's safe down there.'

'Cordelia—'

'No arguments. You've lost one hand and three friends. Do you want to lose more?'

'I'd rather not lose my daughter and her Waymaster.'

'Yeah, still Jay, not Waymaster. And you should have thought of that before you called us in, instead of, say, the cavalry. Off we go. You stay put.'

I got up and headed deeper into the cave before Mother Dearest could muster any further objections. She was weak. No way could she keep up with us.

'Ves,' said Jay from behind me. 'Ves, slow down.'

I did, slightly. 'What's up?'

'Didn't you hear your mother? Three people have died down there this week. How about we don't go marching heedlessly in and get ourselves killed, too?'

I took a breath, and stopped. 'Right. Sorry. Lost my perspective for a moment there.'

'The Vespers do have that effect on people.'

To that, I raised a single brow.

'Never mind. About that hell of a plan you mentioned?'

'Shields.' I began there, mustering strong wards to shroud Jay and I against whatever we might find below. They wouldn't stop a lindworm in full charge, or have much effect on its teeth. But, mother hadn't said what species of worm it was. Poison-spitters were bad news, but my wards should take care of that.

'Pipes.' I retrieved them — Jay politely averted his eyes — and held them ready.

'What do I do?' said Jay. 'You seem to have this covered.'

'Still got that Wand?' I said, referring to the Ruby one he'd been loaned from Stores.

He pulled it from his pocket, handling it tenderly. 'Check.'

I withdrew my Sunstone Wand, too, and held it high. 'In that case: prepare for battle.'

'Battle. Huh.' Jay visibly squared his shoulders, and wielded his pretty Wand in his fist, point down, as though he might stab someone with it. 'I don't know if I've ever mentioned, but battle isn't quite my forte—'

'Learn quickly,' I said over my shoulder, being already in motion again. I summoned a few more fireballs, and let them drift ahead of me like a parade of wisp-lights, leading us down into the darkness. 'You do, in this job.'

'I'm beginning to see that,' Jay muttered, but he caught up with me and kept pace, and we descended together.

The stone-walled passage spiralled steeply down, soon growing damp, earthy and chilly. For a little while, the prevailing silence led me to think that my mother's report still held: the lindworm had vanished through its gateway and had not come back.

Then, after a few minutes of steady descent, a faint sound reached my ears: a distant whisper, *shhhkk,* as of something scaly sliding over stone.

'About learning quickly,' I whispered to Jay. 'Lesson in self-defence imminent.'

Jay lifted his Wand high. 'I hope you're ready with those pipes.'

3

Humble proportions marked the space below; no soaring Mines of Moria halls here. Low ceilings; curving packed-earth walls neatly fitted with cut stones; rounded walls and sloping floors; all marked the caverns beneath Sheep Island as a gnome habitation.

Jay and I stepped, with great caution, into a central hall with three arches leading into shadow-darkened chambers beyond. We kept our backs to the wall, alert for further sounds of the lindworm's approach.

Nothing moved.

'Any of those arches could be the gateway,' I said to Jay in an undertone.

'How do you tell?'

'You don't. Well, you do, but only by what you might call the "reckless" way.'

'Step through and hope?'

'Yup.'

Another dry rasp of scales against stone interrupted my thought, and I froze. Seconds passed as those sounds drew nearer, and nearer still — then the lindworm appeared, writhing sinuously across the worn stones of the floor. More serpent than dragon, its hide gleamed mottled green in my firelight. It had wings, after all, but they were feeble, stunted things, folded against its muscular sides; by no means could it fly with such miserable specimens.

Its blunt-nosed head turned in our direction, its mouth opening to display long, bone-pale fangs. My pipes were at my lips in an instant, my lungs inhaling for a blast of song — but away turned the lindworm's head and on it went, vanishing back into the darkness.

I stood, frozen and unbreathing, for some time before at last I let out a breath. The creature was big enough almost to fill the chamber from floor to ceiling. With such bulk, and such teeth, I considered my mother fortunate to have lost only a hand.

Jay looked enquiringly at me.

'Need to find out where that damned gateway is,' I murmured.

'So we follow?'

'We follow.'

We crept away from the dubious protection of the shadowed wall, and passed under the round-topped arch through which the lindworm had disappeared. To my surprise, the chamber beyond was smaller still than the hall; round-walled, like the rest, bare of furniture, and primitive, it was primarily marked by a lack of two important things: one gigantic lindworm, and any other entrance or exit besides the one through which we had just ventured.

We stood in the centre of the room, momentarily dumbfounded.

'Doesn't a gateway require, you know, a gate?' said Jay after a while.

'Or a doorway, or an arch? You would think so...' I brightened my fireballs until the room glowed in the light, but this had little effect save to confirm the total lack of alternative doorways. Stone-packed walls, unbroken and featureless, met my confused gaze.

'The thing is,' I said, turning in yet another circle, 'we can't do gateways anymore. Not the kind my mother means. Those are among the many arts we've lost, probably forever, and since so few functioning gates have survived down the ages, we know too little about how they work.'

'In other words, maybe it doesn't have to be a door.'

'I suppose not, looking at this. But what, then? There's nothing here.'

Jay reached the nearest wall in two long strides, and laid a hand against it. 'There has to be something.'

I followed suit, selecting the opposite wall, and we groped our way around the room until we'd each covered half. Nothing promising had happened on my side; every-thing under my hands felt cold, solid and immoveable, as stone should.

Jay shook his head in response to my questioning look. 'Nothing.'

I hovered, undecided. 'We could wait for the lindworm to come back, and see where it comes from. But that could take hours, and I'm worried about my mother.'

'I don't suppose she would submit to being taken to hospital, if we're stymied?'

'I know you've spent only ten minutes in her company, but what do you think is the answer to that question?'

'Forget it?'

'Mm. She'll camp here until she either succeeds or dies.'

Jay's eyebrows flickered. He has an expressive face. I'm still building up my mental dictionary of what all these fas-cinating expressions mean, but I think that eyebrow-shim-my indicated he'd had several thoughts in response to my comment and was disposed to air none of them.

Probably a good thing.

I retreated to the lone arch through which we had entered. 'We'd better get out of the way. When the worm comes back—'

Gods, the thing just *erupted* out of the wall like a scaled explosion, teeth snapping. Jay leapt out of its way with a startled shout, and lost a bit of his jacket to a snap of the lindworm's jaws. He barrelled into me, swept me up, and rocketed away with the beast hard behind him.

I writhed.

'Stop it,' panted Jay.

'Need my arm— can't— there!' I got my pipes to my lips and played, brisk and loudly. I used much the same melody that had pacified those griffins, upon our first adventure into Farringale, though at a greater tempo, and with urgent flourishes like bursts of trumpets. These last visibly affected the lindworm, for with each little explosion of sound, it flinched.

We ran out of hall to flee through, and hit the wall. Jay, bless him, released me and turned, Wand raised, facing down the oncoming worm with the kind of courage hero's tales are made out of. You know, the kind they sing over your funeral bier. I don't know what he thought he was going to do. I don't think he did either.

I got in his way. One advantage to a certain lack of size is nimbleness; a twist and a jump and I managed to insert myself between Jay and those jaws. Having both arms free once more, I held the pipes to my lips with one hand — still playing furiously — and raised my Sunstone Wand with the other. I'm not great at fireballs, but if you spit streams of them into a foe's wide-open eyes they tend to have an impact, even if they're the approximate size of a two pound coin.

The lindworm roared and reared back, shaking its head. Flame rippled over its face, searing its mottled scales. Thankfully, its terrible onslaught stopped.

'Ves, you *idiot*,' snarled Jay, but he got the idea. A second stream of fireballs, these green and rather bigger than mine, joined the assault, leaving me free to focus on the song.

I did that, amplifying its effects and hastening its impact with every scrap of magick at my disposal. It took too, too long, while the lindworm snapped at Jay and at me in (mercifully) blind rage; but at length the creature's movements slowed, its jaw slackened, and it sagged.

Jay let the stream of fireballs gradually die. The lindworm stayed where it was, swaying slightly, but otherwise motionless.

I cast a frantic look at Jay, trying to signal with my eyes: *Can you do that thing your sister did and get the stones to hold it?*

His only response was a helpless look at our featureless environs, which I took to mean: *no.*

Which left me to play indefinitely, facing down a temporarily-pacified lindworm for, potentially, eternity.

For once, I agreed with Jay: I really ought to have thought out the details of this one a bit sooner.

To my dismay, Jay made *wait here* motions with his hands — honestly, where did he think I was going to go? — and ran away.

I played on, clammy with sweat. The combination of exertion, fear and too many fireballs at close proximity will do that, even to a fine lady like myself.

In blessedly few minutes I heard the oncoming thud of Jay's returning footsteps. When he came back into view, firelight spinning around his head, he had my mother in his arms. She had the grim, suffering look of a woman in great pain, but who'd be damned if she would admit to it.

He jerked his head in the direction of the mysterious chamber which had, somehow, facilitated the vanishing and reappearance of the lindworm, and departed that way at a near run.

I went more slowly, playing, playing, beginning to hate every trilling note that soared from my pipes. Beautiful pipes, wretched pipes, how fervently I wished to cease the strain upon my burning lungs, and put the pretty things down!

But I followed Jay and my mother, stepping carefully backwards, keeping my eyes fixed on the looming shape of the lindworm. Soon I felt Jay's hands grabbing at my shoulders, guiding me none too gently into the cramped chamber.

'Your mother's figured it out,' he said, breathlessly. He pulled me inexorably backwards. As I was facing the wrong way, ever vigilant against the worm, I do not know at what point I went through the wall. I felt nothing, at any rate. I only became aware that, all of a sudden, I could no longer see the lindworm; a solid wall blocked my view of the chamber we'd so lately gone through.

I permitted myself to play a little more slowly, pausing occasionally to draw great lungsful of air. I dared not stop altogether, yet. We had already received ample proof of the worm's ability to pass through the wall-gate at will, and I did not know how long my song would hold it once the final notes died away.

I did, however, turn to survey where we had ended up.

We were in a storeroom, though largely empty of contents. Much larger in proportion than the rooms we had just left, this room had a high ceiling and white-washed walls, though both were liberally draped in dusty cobwebs. Shelves ran from floor to just below the ceiling, some of them still bearing aged oak barrels.

The far wall was missing. Well, not all of it; half, perhaps, lay tumbled in stony fragments over the floor, exactly as though a lindworm, say, had broken through it.

Jay had set my mother down against one wall, and now stood guard over her, Wand raised. A tiny fireball blossomed at its tip, ready to fire.

'Mother,' I said, in between notes. 'Functional?'

'Breathing.'

'What did you do?'

'To the wall? Sang to it.'

Lacking breath for further conversation, I said nothing, but my eyebrows said: *what?* eloquently enough.

'Ludovic Deschain's Songs of Opening and Entry, chapter six.'

I wondered how the lindworm had managed the process. Did serpents sing? But that was a question for another time.

'Let's move on,' said Jay, watching me. Perhaps he was motivated by the beads of sweat pouring down my face. 'Sooner we get somewhere the lindworm can't follow, the better.'

I managed to nod frantically.

He scooped up mother again, and we went en masse to the make-shift door the lindworm had created for itself. We moved two abreast; encumbered as Jay was with my mother, and distracted as I was by the music I still played, neither of us was best positioned to tackle any new threats. What if there was more than one lindworm down here?

Thankfully, we did not encounter any more. Beyond the storeroom lay the partially-wrecked remains of expansive cellars, some parts of which still contained dust-grimed bottles of some long forgotten beverage. Nothing stirred.

'I can walk,' snarled my mother at one point.

'But not quickly,' said Jay. I thought it fortunate for him that the Vesper women were none of us tall, or he'd have been prostrated by now.

Having put some significant distance between us, the wall-gate and the lindworm beyond, I finally permitted my song to fade away in favour of gasping in air.

'You okay?' said Jay.

'Kind of,' I panted. 'Where are we?'

'No clue.'

We found dark stone stairs and went up them, slowly and cautiously, ears straining for any sound of habitation. None came. As we emerged from the stairwell into a darkened hall beyond, the sudden feeling of openness and air told me, though my eyes lacked the light to confirm it, that we had entered something spacious — possibly grand.

Moments later, lights flared into life, searing my unprepared eyes until they wept protesting tears.

What I saw took my breath again.

Remember that crack about Moria? What we'd stumbled into wasn't too far off. A great, wide, echoing hallway lay before us, walls of silvered stone flying so, so high.

Bright globes of light adorned the tops of mighty, graceful pillars running in twin rows down the centre of the hall. The ceiling, what I could see of it, was painted with murals the colour of moss and amethyst; long, darkened windows glittered sombrely in the pale, intense light.

'Right,' croaked Jay, and almost dropped Mother. 'Uh. Where are we?'

'If I'm not mistaken,' I said, drifting a step or two farther into the hall, 'we're in what the non-magickers might call fairyland.'

4

'WHY DO I FEEL like this isn't going to be nearly as nice as it sounds?' said Jay.

Fairyland does sound lovely, doesn't it? The word conjures up sweet, diminutive creatures with gossamer wings, flower gowns and stars in their hair, living in buttercup houses and feasting upon ambrosia and honey.

Most of this is nonsense. Look farther back; listen to the tales the trees tell, that the lakes and the stones remember. The Fair Folk, as they are always called in their various ways, are as diverse — and, in their own ways, as destructive — as humankind. Tolkien made bright, noble heroes of them, and sometimes that is exactly what they are. Sometimes (as with humans), the fair façade hides a rotten core.

If one is unwise or unlucky enough to set foot in Fairyland, one ought to remember this simple principle: tread with infinite care.

Having feasted my eyes upon the seductive beauty of that echoing hall, I turned them, with less satisfaction, upon my mother. She, alone of the three of us, did not seem surprised. Nor did she seem either sufficiently awed or sufficiently wary for my taste. 'Mother, dear,' I said. 'Would you like to tell us what we are doing here?'

She looked sideways at me, a shifty look if ever I saw one. 'Why, we are here to explore.'

'By accident or by design?'

She gave a short, huffy sigh, and looked up at the ceiling. 'Always so suspicious.'

'Rightly so, in this case?'

'Yes, if you must know.'

'I thought you were on Sheep Island looking for a lost gnome village.'

'So we were. But the fact that we were doing so in Cumbria was not by chance. I've devoted years to digs across this county, hoping that, one day, I'd find a way back.'

'A way *back*? You've been here before?'

'When I was approximately your age.'

I gave a sigh, too, and sat down near to her. Jay stood looming over us, hands on his hips, glowering in a way that ought to have disconcerted my mother if she had an ounce of feeling about her.

She didn't.

'Where are we?' I demanded of her.

'We are in the halls of the Tylwyth Teg, specifically one of the kingdoms of the Yllanfalen,' said my maddening parent. 'At least, I hope we are. It looks right.' She cast another glance up at the long windows, through which twilight and starlight softly shone. 'More specifically than that I couldn't yet say, but I *hope* we're in Ygranyllon.'

'Is Ygranyllon deserted?' I said, casting a meaningful look at the echoing emptiness around us. 'If so, I'd say the signs are favourable.'

'Parts of it. Their monarchy fell when King Evelaern passed, and for reasons best known to themselves they have never chosen another. They live principally out in the valleys, now, and edifices such as this are used only for occasions of ceremony.'

I nodded along with growing impatience. 'Very well; and why did you want to come back here?'

'Those pipes,' she said, looking suddenly at me. 'Do you know anything about them, Cordelia?'

'I know that they are classified as a Great Treasure, and that they are accounted too precious for the likes of me,' I answered, feeling obscurely nettled. 'But I received them from the hand — so to speak — of a unicorn, and since

Milady has always been in favour of their remaining with me, I do not consider myself an unworthy guardian.'

'I do not question your right of ownership,' said my mother, rolling her eyes. 'I asked if you *know* anything about them.'

I took a breath, counselling myself to patience. 'I know that they saved our backsides from the lindworm just now, and from griffins before that. They've performed similarly at other times, in the past. But principally I use them to summon Addie.'

Her head tilted at that, questioning.

'Adeline. The unicorn who gave them to me. She brings friends, sometimes, if I ask her to.'

'Has it not occurred to you how absurdly rare it is to have the power to whistle up a unicorn? Or how absurdly blessed you are in possessing it?'

'Frequently.' And it had, but not so much in recent years. I suppose I had grown used to it, and I ought not have.

Mother cast another, long-suffering look towards the ceiling. 'There is an old story in these parts,' she began afresh. 'About a pair of Treasures of extraordinary power, wrought by the hand of King Evelaern himself. One was a lyre, made from something they called moonsilver and strung with enchanted waters from the King's own pools. And the other, Cordelia, was a set of syrinx pipes crafted from skysilver, said to have the power to whistle up the winds themselves.'

I blinked. 'Uh… oh.'

'Oh indeed. While I have no proof that the pipes which, so fortuitously, fell into your hands ten years ago, are the same as King Evelaern's skysilver syrinx, I consider it highly probable. For the Tylwyth Teg were known for the close fellowship they enjoyed with the species we call unicorns.'

'Uh.'

'Furthermore,' she said with a quelling look at me, 'King Evelaern had a principle mount, long ago, or so the stories said. The unicorn of his particular choice was an ethereal creature, pale of hide and hoof, said to shine, at times, like skysilver itself. Now I grant you, white or silvery unicorns are hardly uncommon in folklore. Nonetheless, does not something about this description strike you as familiar?'

I could only nod wordlessly around the dropping sensation in my stomach.

Giddy gods, was Adeline used to hobnobbing with fae royalty? What in the world had she been doing all these years hanging around with *me*?

I cleared my dry throat. 'She likes chips,' I offered.

'What.'

'Adeline. If that's any help.'

Mother levelled a cool look at me. 'Does it appear likely to you that ancient legend and song might find occasion to mention the King's Mount's fondness for chips?'

I had to grin at that, inappropriate though it was. 'If they didn't, they should have.'

'I will submit your corrections to the bards.'

'Right, then,' interrupted Jay. 'If I'm following your line of thinking correctly, we're here for the lyre.'

'I caught a glimpse of it, I believe,' said my mother, with a wistful note unusual for her. 'Just the once. It looks like... well, if we are lucky, we will all find out what it looks like in some detail, soon enough.'

'Why's it so important?' said Jay, rather sternly. 'As grateful as I am for Ves's pipes, as they have indeed saved our behinds, is this lyre worth the deaths of your friends?'

My mother's eyes flashed fire at that. 'If you imagine, Mr. Patel, that I do not bitterly regret those losses, or that I shall not continue to reproach myself for their deaths for as long as I shall live, you are much mistaken.'

Jay spoke in a softened tone. 'I did not mean to imply any such thing.'

She clenched her jaw, and took a few moments to speak again. 'We had no warning of the lindworm. We've never encountered such a beast anywhere in Cumbria before, we heard no rumours of such... it was a terrible, awful misfortune. But.' Her voice hardened. 'I shall not be deterred. If they died for this quest, then I must finish it. Anything less would be a disgrace.'

I wanted to point out that she had very nearly honoured Hank's memory by feeding *us* to a lindworm straight after, but something about my mother's expression stopped me. Her eyes were too bright.

Delia Vesper never, *ever* cries.

I looked around at all the chill stone and glass surrounding us, at its undeniable beauty and its aching loneliness, and sighed. 'I'll say again, Mother, I wish you'd told me some of this on the phone. I would've brought Pup with me, too.' Having no notion of what to expect when we tracked down my wayward parent, I had elected to leave my disgraceful Robin Goodfellow with Alban. I didn't want her getting into the kind of trouble that might prove permanently detrimental to her health. But now I regretted it, for who better to help us track down a priceless mythical lyre?

I expected some enquiry as to the identity of Pup, and when none came I grew suspicious again. Just how much had Milady told her about my recent doings?

Why did the possibility aggravate me?

'I was pressed for time,' she said instead, and waved her arm at me — the one with a ragged, lividly cauterised stump where her hand used to be. 'I was still bleeding.'

I shuddered.

'Right,' I said, climbing to my feet. I'd left my satchel behind, too, for similar reasons, and in contrast I was glad of it, for I'd probably have fallen on and broken half the contents by now. I'd brought only a small belt-bag with me, in which I'd stashed my Sunstone Wand, and a few of those restorative phials and such that Rob had given me prior to our adventure into Farringale. I extracted one, a delicate, curved glass bottle filled with a lazily swirling greenish liquid, and gave it to my mother. 'Get that down you,' I instructed. 'Ophelia made it, and she's our best concoctionist. It should set you up for a bit of proper, old-fashioned questing.'

Mother tossed back the elixir, grimacing at its flavour. 'I never understand why these miraculous potions cannot also taste halfway decent.'

'Grumble, grumble. How do you feel?'

'About half alive, which is an improvement.'

'Super. As a note to the group, I've got only one more of those, so let's not get ourselves mostly-deaded, hm?'

'Yes, ma'am.' Jay gave me a tiny salute. 'What's our inventory otherwise?'

'Not much else,' I said.

He did that thing with his eyebrows, the sceptical/long-suffering thing. 'Honestly. You haul half the contents of Home around for almost every assignment we've been on — except this one, when we actually need it?'

'I thought we were just paying a visit to my mother. Tea and a cosy chat, remember? Did you bring anything useful with you?'

'Wand.'

'Me too.'

'And… that's it.' He grinned sheepishly. 'I always assume you've got everything.'

'Ah well. Whatever we can't manage to accomplish with two Wands between us is probably not worth doing.'

'Not to mention,' said Mother, hauling herself awkwardly to her feet, 'King Evelaern's skysilver pipes. Which,' she added, frowning at me, 'you appear to have been keeping in your bra.'

'They've been safe there,' I said, rather lamely.

'They should be displayed in splendour and security at the House.'

'But then they wouldn't be doing anyone any good.'

'They would be doing the Society a great deal of good.'

'And I'd probably be dead by now.'

'Doubtful. Your reliance on those pipes makes you reckless. You'd be less so, if you didn't have a Great Treasure to get you out of trouble.'

I gave her a sideways look of my own. 'It's been six years since we last spoke, Mother. How do you know?'

She looked, I thought, faintly sheepish herself, and gave a stamp with one booted foot. 'Hmph. Let's get on, shall we? Before that lindworm comes back for another helping.'

5

In all my decade at the Society, I don't think I've ever been on a proper, old-fashioned hero quest before. Deserted halls! Monsters! An artefact of great power!

Course, when Frodo and Sam set out to destroy the ring, they numbered nine, and one of them was some kind of a demigod. In our Quest for the Lyre we numbered but three, and one of us was half-dead and missing body parts.

At least we weren't heading into Mordor.

Hopefully.

'Right, then,' I said, wand and pipes at the ready. 'Where's the lyre?'

'Good question,' said mother.

'I thought you said you'd seen them?'

'Years ago, and the circumstances were unusual.'

'Namely?'

'Well.' Mother seemed absorbed in the study of her right toe. 'The Yllanfalen hold *great* parties.'

'Parties.' I think my eyebrows did that sceptical-Jay thing. 'Did I hear that right?'

'Last time I set foot in these halls, they were celebrating some kind of summer festival. Music, feasting, etc. A man with eyes like spun clouds was playing the most extraordinary lyre...' Mother trailed off, apparently lost in memory.

I waited.

'That music,' said Mother at last. 'I've never heard its like, before or since. It could move the world.' She gave a tiny smile, and added, 'The lyre-player wasn't half bad either.'

'*Mother.*'

'Sorry. Well, I may have somewhat over imbibed on the ambrosia and nectar, and fallen asleep under a table somewhere. When I woke, everyone was gone. In fact, the place was pristine — you wouldn't think hundreds of fae had spent the night there in high revelry. All that was left was me, the wind, and the headache from hell.'

'You aren't telling me you've spent, what, two decades trying to find your way back to a party.'

'Three,' said Mother.

'Three decades?'

'A little more, even.'

'For a *party*?'

She disconcerted me by drawing her arm out of her coat and clinically inspecting the stump where her hand once was. 'It was a bit more important than that.'

Jay looked hard at my mother, and then, rather narrowly, at me.

'What?' I said to him.

'Nothing. So this party. Whereabouts was it, exactly? Is this the same place?'

'How should I know?' said Mother.

'As the only one of the three of us who's set foot in here before—'

'Once, thirty years ago. Actually no, that's not quite true. I found another portal this one other time, but it led into some kind of mausoleum or something and there were no other exits. So, close enough.'

'Well,' I said, suppressing a sigh. 'We can go looking for the lyre, or we can go looking for the lyre-player.'

Mother looked quickly at me.

'What? People are probably going to be easier to track down than an inanimate object of unknown location. And since we're here with little equipment and no food, finding something resembling civilisation might not be a bad idea anyway.'

'You said they live out in the valleys?' Jay said.

'Typically,' said Mother.

'If these buildings are still used for ceremonies, the revellers probably aren't all that far away. Let's find a way out.' Jay marched off with that lovely, purposeful stride of his.

'And if we do find them?' my mother called, hastening after him. 'What then? Greetings, fair folk, we come to pinch your lyre, would you mind just handing it over?'

'Who said anything about pinching it?' Jay threw over his shoulder. 'We'll take a look at it, they'll tell us this particular model is not for sale, and we'll go home.'

I trotted after the pair of them. 'I'm not sure that's going to satisfy Mum,' I called.

'It will have to.'

I'D LOVE TO SAY that we wandered up and down dale (or hallway, in this instance), and happened conveniently upon a faerie town in no time at all. But when is life ever anything less than supremely complicated? We wandered and we wandered and we turned ourselves in circles. I can't say I disliked this entirely, for wherever it was we'd got to was spectacularly beautiful. I could well believe it to have been a royal palace at one time, for it had all the necessary splendour, and the kind of ethereal glory one sees only in faerie halls. Windows twinkled like frosted starlight; bejewelled leaves on airy vines twined in vivid lustre around slender white pillars, and carpeted the floor; one chamber was devoted entirely to a shallow, serene pool of twilight-blue water, its bed littered with delicate, pearly shells.

What we never found, however, included such ordinary arrangements as, say, kitchens. Either the Yllanfalen did not eat (which, by my mother's accounts of revelry, seemed unlikely), or such mundanities were banished to the lower levels, with the storerooms. None of us wanted to go down there again, if we did not have to.

We didn't find a way out, either. The nearest thing to it was a turret, high up in the northwest corner (so Jay said, I have no idea how he could tell). We toiled up spiralling stairs and came out at last into fresh, balmy air, all silvered, somehow, and colder than it ought by right to be. Before us lay valleys and hills, as my mother had said, but nothing so ordinary would do for a Faerie Dell. Starry meadows awaited us, strewn with flowers; fronded trees hung with clear lights gathered in copses here and there; and the sky had a tinge of green to it, like cool jade.

'Nice,' said Jay.

'Understatement of the century,' said I.

He shrugged. 'My eyes have been out on stalks for hours. I'm jaded.'

I turned about, and spotted, in the distance, a scant shadow on the horizon that might have been a town. 'People, ahoy!' I said, and pointed.

'Maybe.' Jay scrutinised the view. 'Want to help me shift some chairs up here?'

'Up those stairs? Not really.' The steps in question were narrow, cramped and twirly.

'Come on.' Jay took my arm and unceremoniously towed me after him.

'Be right back, Mother,' I said with a sigh.

Ten minutes and quite a bit of swearing later, we had three freshly-witched chairs assembled at the top of the turret. They weren't our first choices. When flying, it's always best to choose big, solid specimens if you can, with arms to cling to. These were delicate, with narrow seats and spindly legs. Decorative but deadly.

Needs must.

'We'd better take it slowly,' said Jay. 'And keep your mother between us. She's only got one hand to hang on with.'

'Righto.' I took hold of the tall back of mother's chair with one hand, and Jay did the same. Up we went, and over.

It's odd, perspective. As long as we were safely tucked behind the wall ringing the turret's top, it didn't look so very far to the ground. Once we had jumped over that barrier and cast ourselves upon the mercy of the winds, the ground seemed so terribly far away. I tried not to watch as it came closer and closer, my stomach clenching, my mouth dry, gripping my mother's chair with all my might. Giddy gods, what if she fell off? What if *I* fell off?

Nobody fell off. At least, not until we had landed with an inelegant crash, and then we all fell off. At least we only had a foot or two to fall, by then.

'All in one piece?' I said, directing most of my solicitude to my mother, bashed up as she already was.

'As close to it as I'll ever get again,' answered Mother.

Right. I picked up the chairs. 'I think we'd better fly, or it'll take us all day to reach that town. But we can stay low.'

'I'm curious,' said Jay. 'Did you ever try this trick on a carpet?'

'Yes.'

'And?'

'You know how difficult it was not to fall off your chair just now?'

'I remember it vividly.'

'And you know how carpets have nothing to hold on to?'

'Right.'

'And you know how carpets aren't at all solid and tend to flop all over the place?'

'I see your point.'

'It looks cute on screen, but in reality it's a suicide mission.'

'Chairs it is.'

Chairs it was, for an exhausting trip up the gentle but significant slope of an expansive hill. Its carpet of feathered grasses tickled my legs and made my mother sneeze. A few droplets of rain sailed down upon us from an almost cloudless sky, much to my puzzlement, and I shivered in my thin summer blouse. My right arm ached abominably from clinging on to my mother's enchanted conveyance, and I could not help noticing the greyish tinge to her face. I was grateful beyond measure when we drew close enough to that shadow on the horizon to be certain of its identity as a town.

'Let's stop here,' I said, when we were still some little distance away.

'Why?' snapped Mother.

'Safe distance. The fae are tricky sometimes.'

'I spent a whole night with them and emerged unscathed.'

'You spent a whole night listening to their music and eating their food, and thirty years later you're still trying to get back. Does that sound like "unscathed" to you?'

My mother went uncharacteristically quiet.

'And you'll note I politely glossed over the whole missing hand thing.'

'Fine.' Mother sighed. 'What do you propose to do?'

I fished out King Evelaern's skysilver pipes, if that's what they were. 'I thought I'd see if the fine folk over there would like these back.'

'*What?*'

I was already off and striding, brandishing the pipes like a weapon. 'I don't know how they came to lose them, but if they're as fond of that lyre as you suggest, I'd say they would be interested in getting a look at these.'

'Cordelia—'

'And when I tell them where I got them, and whistle up Adeline-and-friends to boot, I'd say we'll be in business.'

'Ves,' sighed Jay.

I stopped at that. 'Yes?'

'You remember what your mother *just* said about those pipes and being reckless?'

I looked doubtfully at my pretty pipes. Glory. They *did* sparkle so beautifully in the faerie light. 'You think she might have had a point?'

'I think it just possible.'

I nodded slowly, thinking that over. 'Ah well,' I said with a shrug, and went off again.

'Ves—'

'At least there aren't any lindworms out here,' I called back.

'Ves! You can't give away your pipes!'

'I said I'd see if they want them back. I didn't say I'd hand them over.'

'Oh, for—' Whatever else Jay said was lost under a stream of muttered curses.

'Have you two been working together long?' I heard my mother say to Jay.

'Nope.'

'How long would you say it'll be before you run screaming for the hills?'

'About the middle of next week.'

'I love you too,' I retorted, and lifted my pipes to my lips. The moment I blew the first note, I knew something was different. The melody shimmered upon the air, expanded, soared; I felt it in every bone.

The Dell responded. The grasses blew up around my feet; birds descended from the skies, and hovered around me; an echo of the song built in the earth and stones beneath my feet, and thrummed along.

A rustle in the grass revealed the presence of squirrels, mice and other small meadow-creatures dashing along in my train.

Jay uttered another curse. 'Great,' he sighed. 'Now she's a sodding Disney princess.'

6

AND SO, WE WENT rolling up to the distant Yllanfalen town with an entourage of meadowlands creatures and a mantle of magickal music. One of the more exhilarating experiences of my life, without a doubt.

Shame that our arrival met with only the echoing silence of deserted streets.

Not *quite* empty, in fact, but close. The silvery gates stood open; we entered a pretty, ancient town, its buildings as tall, slender and elegant as the few inhabitants we saw. I've rarely seen a more verdant settlement, either: climbing vines clambered up every wall, twined with relish around chimney-pots and window frames, and carpeted some part of the stone-cobbled streets to boot. Many of them were in full bloom as well, opening flurries of azure, lavender or ice-white flowers to the sun. The place smelled heavenly.

But it was not populous. We travelled the length of one narrow, winding street before we saw anybody at all, and then we saw only a woman going into what appeared to be a shop. She barely glanced at me, in all my magickal glory.

When the next few people we passed exhibited the same utter lack of interest, I gave up playing.

'Well,' said Jay. 'That was unexpected.'

I nodded, feeling crestfallen and trying not to show it. Honestly, who were these people? Did colourful young women so often prance through the town, wafted on a tide of magick and melody and pursued by an entourage of adoring creatures? Surely not. I couldn't believe it, not even of a place one might reasonably term a part of Faerie.

Jay elbowed me. 'Ves.'

I looked where he was pointing. A lady came towards us down the street — definitely a *lady*, not just a woman, for she was draped in the finest fabric money and magick can procure, and walked with the grace of a queen. She was decked in jewels to a degree bordering upon tasteless, at that.

Of all her ornaments, it was her necklace that caught, and held, my attention, for strung on prominent display upon a light silver chain was a set of tiny syrinx pipes. Hers were the colour of brass, not silver like mine, but in every other respect they were identical.

'Um,' I said. 'Mother?'

Mother dearest stood in silence for a while, watching the ethereal lady pass. Her face registered something very like personal offence.

I kid you not, tiny flowers bloomed where the lady's feet had lately trod.

'Okay,' I said. 'What's the Faerie Queene doing wandering the streets of an Yllanfalen backwater all by herself?'

'I told you,' said Mother. 'They have no monarchs anymore.'

'Are you sure? Because you don't seem to have seen the duplicate-pipes thing comi—' I broke off because Jay elbowed me again. 'Ow. What?'

'Incoming,' he said, turning me around to face a side-alley adjoining the street upon which we stood. There came another denizen of Faerie, a man this time, wearing long jewel-green robes. He had stars in his hair and magick in his eyes and he, too, bore a set of syrinx pipes on a ribbon around his neck. Gold, this time.

I groaned. 'New plan?'

My mother looked from my silvery pipes to the gold ones worn by the Faerie-King-Who-Probably-Wasn't, and sighed. 'It's just possible these aren't King Evelaern's pipes after all,' she allowed.

'You think?'

The next half-hour confirmed the hypothesis beyond doubt, for we found every inhabitant of that impossible town to be as dripping in grace and glory as those early few, and many of them had pipes. Too many.

'What the bloody hell is this place?' said Jay after a while. 'These people are unreal.'

I had to agree. I'm not given to feelings of inadequacy, but when you're a plain, ordinary human (fabulously magickal hair excepted) surrounded by such ethereally beautiful beings, it is difficult to help feeling somewhat diminished.

Even my mother felt it, what with her filthy clothes and hair and her wounded arm. That's saying something. Mother is usually impervious to such trifles as appearance.

'Enough dithering,' I said after a while, having arrived at a central square dominated by a lofty white clocktower. 'I'm going to ask—' I stopped. An open doorway to my left offered a peek into a small shop premises, what probably passed for humble in this peculiar place. Hanging from the rafters was an array of tiny objects which sparkled in the sun.

I veered inside.

'These pipes,' I said to the proprietor.

'Yes?' She was rather taller than me, and (to my chagrin) much better dressed. I was wearing baggy trousers and trekking boots; she wore a flowing sky-coloured gown with trailing ribbons, an array of starry jewels, and she had fireflies glimmering in her hair.

Gods damnit.

'What are they?' I said, waving my own about. 'Why does everybody have them?'

She looked me over in a none too friendly fashion, then turned her attention to Mother, and Jay. 'Visitors?' was all she said.

'As you see.'

'And how did you come here?'

Jay and I swapped a look that said, *cripes, good question.*

So it fell to Mother to say: 'Through the Old King's Halls.'

The ethereal goddess's interest sharpened. 'And how came you there? Those halls have long been closed.'

'Through a portal. Don't worry, it is well hidden in Britain proper. No one's going to find it.'

'Except for you.'

'Well. I was looking rather hard.'

The proprietor's forbidding frown did not in the smallest degree lessen — until she looked again at my pipes. 'How came you by *those*? It is too much to imagine that anybody gave them to you.'

'Someone did, in a manner of speaking,' I said. 'Just not today.'

Apparently tired of wasting words on me, the lady merely raised one pale brow.

'A unicorn,' I supplied.

'A unicorn,' she repeated.

'Yes.'

'Gave a rare set of skysilver pipes to a human.'

I was beginning to feel that these beauteous people were somewhat xenophobic. 'That's right. Ten years ago, or thereabouts.'

'Eleven,' said Mother.

'What?'

'It was eleven years ago.'

'How do you know? You only found out like, last week—'

Mother directed a quelling look at me, effectively shutting me up. 'I've known for a while.'

'I—'

'Can you play them?' interrupted the lady.

I blinked. 'Of course I can play them. Do you think any halfway sane witch would just sit on a Treasure like these for eleven years?'

She folded her arms, silent. Her look said: *oh really?*

So I played.

'Ves,' sighed Jay after about twenty seconds. 'You're not seriously— that isn't—'

He gave up.

I played on. What, I'm compelled to play faerie music or something? What's wrong with John Farnham? I'd got halfway through the chorus of *You're the Voice* when the lady waved a hand. 'Enough.'

I played a few bars of Tears for Fears, but didn't get as far as the chorus as she growled, 'Stop!' and glared at me.

I stopped.

'You play well,' she said, possibly through gritted teeth.

I checked her perfect ears for signs of bleeding. Nope.

'So, the pipes?' I said. 'We've scarcely seen a soul who wasn't wearing a set.'

'We are a musical society.'

'I guessed that much.'

'Could King Evelaern's pipes really call up the winds?' said my mother abruptly.

The proprietor looked sharply at Mother. 'So the stories say.'

'You don't know for sure?'

'They have not been played since the King's passing.' Her eyes strayed to the pipes in my hand, as did mine. I began to doubt again. Were these the King's pipes? Had they passed out of Yllanfalen knowledge because Addie had been keeping them? 'It is possible that the winds responded to the King's magick, rather than the pipes,' she continued, without commenting upon mine.

'Perhaps that's so,' agreed Mother affably.

The proprietor-lady smiled, for the first time. 'We have a fine range of music for syrinx pipes,' she said, and glided away to an oak-wrought rack filled with sheet music scribed elegantly upon thick paper. 'Perhaps you would enjoy expanding your repertoire?'

A sales pitch? Seriously? I was about to say no, but Mother forestalled me. 'Delightful,' she said firmly, and to my surprise fished a quantity of silvery coins out of a pocket in her begrimed trousers. They were no type of currency I'd ever seen, but she poured half of them into the proprietor's hands and they were accepted with a gracious nod. 'Might you have some recommendations for my daughter's interest?'

'Certainly.' The lady extended her slender, perfect hands and selected a few sheets. '*Llewellir* is a song for sleep. Very popular with insomniacs. *Syllphyllan*, a favourite with gardeners and orchard-tenders, as the sprites adore it. Ah yes, *Yshllyn Ara Elenaril* is a fine choice, if you are interested in weather magick? I cannot promise the winds, but it has been known to muster a little rain on occasion.' She handed all these to me, and considered the rack for a thoughtful moment. 'One more. *Ellyall dy Iythran,* a song for the stars.'

That last made little sense to me, and as I accepted the page in question from her I opened my mouth to enquire.

'What about lyres?' said Mother, forestalling me. 'Do you sell those?'

'Naturally,' said the gracious proprietor.

'I'm looking for something in moonsilver.'

That sharp look came again. 'You are well informed as to the old tales, aren't you? Only one such lyre was ever made.'

My mother gave a smile I can only describe as sharkish. 'Can I buy that one?'

'It is not for sale.'

'Why not? I have money.'

'I daresay, but none among the Yllanfalen would sell you King Evelaern's Lyre, even if we could.'

Mother's ears pricked up. 'Cannot you?'

'That is lost.'

'But it wasn't lost thir—' Mother stopped.

'Yes?' prompted the lady.

'Nothing.'

I intervened, saying more graciously, 'How did it come to be lost? Is there a story about that?'

'That is not known,' she said.

'Where did it used to be kept?' Mother was insistent.

'In a vault built for the purpose, in those very halls you claim to have but lately exited.' She smiled coolly. 'It is perfectly useless to go there, if that is what is in your minds. The vault is quite empty.'

'Who was the last person to see the lyre?' said Mother, getting right into detective mode.

'I have not the smallest idea.' The proprietor's patience was wearing thin, her smile becoming strained. 'Will that be all?'

'Yes,' I said hastily. 'Thank you. Come along, Mother.'

'A moment,' said the proprietor, halting me in the process of striding out of the shop.

I turned back. 'Yes?'

'I would like to meet the unicorn who gave you those pipes.'

I met her gaze levelly. 'Why?'

'It is a remarkable tale.'

'Also a true one.'

'No doubt.' Her tone suggested she was by no means so convinced as her words implied.

I paused to consider. If I summoned Addie, she would know I spoke the truth; and then what?

No idea. Right, then. Time for another exciting round of *Trial and Error.*

'Come hither, then,' I said, and led the way out of the shop. I've no doubt Adeline would follow me right into the store, and that would be about as successful as ye olde bull-in-a-china-shop scenario.

The moment the sun hit me, I played Addie's song. Just hers, this time; no requests for companions layered in with the melody. I had the satisfaction of seeing our supercilious shopkeeper's face register surprise, even incredulity — and Addie hadn't even shown up yet.

She arrived a few minutes later, spiralling lazily out of a half-clouded sky. Trotting straight up to me, she whickered and bumped me with her soft nose.

'I haven't got any more chips,' I whispered. 'Sorry.'

Adeline gave an unattractive snort.

'Where,' said the proprietor softly, 'did you learn that song?'

I opened my mouth to answer, and realised that I had no idea. 'It was the first song I played,' I said. 'When I first set the pipes to my lips.'

'You had no skill with the syrinx before?'

'I'd never so much as seen a set before.'

'I see.' The lady looked me over slowly, and then gave the same wondering look to pretty Adeline. 'Thank you,' she said, and walked back into her shop.

'I'm not sure what I've just done,' I admitted to Mother and Jay.

'Given her something to think about,' said Mother.

I'd hoped that showing off Addie would have answered a question or two. Was she King Evelaern's favourite mount? Were these extra-super-special-and-magickal pipes or just the common-or-garden, incredibly-rare-and-rather-very-magickal variety? Inquiring minds were not to be satisfied today.

7

'RIGHT, THEN,' I SAID, searching in vain for somewhere to stuff my new collection of music. 'New plan?'

'Find the lyre-thief,' said Mother promptly.

'You think it was stolen?' said Jay.

'Sounds like it.'

'By whom?'

'How should I know?'

Jay did his arms-folded-and-staring thing. 'It occurs to me that you might have been the last person to see that lyre.'

'If I was, why would I be looking for it now?'

'Are you looking for it now?'

'Why else would I be here?'

Jay shrugged.

Mother gave a sigh, and rubbed at her eyes. 'It's possible that it went missing on the night that I saw it,' she allowed. 'But if it did, it certainly wasn't me that took it.' She paused. 'Not that I wouldn't have, given half a chance. It had that effect on people.'

'What effect?' Jay said, looking at Mother intently.

She shrugged. 'You couldn't see it, and hear it played, without wanting it. That's why they kept it in a vault, I suppose.'

'The effect is long-lasting, it seems,' said Jay.

'In that I still want it, three decades later? Mm.'

That noncommittal *mm* at the end sounded off to me. 'Is there anything you haven't told us, Mother dear?' I said. 'Is this only about the lyre?'

'What do you mean?'

I mimicked Jay's folded-arms posture and icy stare. 'What about the lyre-player that you mentioned?'

'Could he have taken it?' said Jay.

Mother spread her hands. 'I don't know. Perhaps he could have.'

'Who is he?' I prompted.

'I never knew his name.'

'That's going to make it pretty difficult to find him, then, isn't it?'

'Few people can play a lyre like that. It can't be that hard to track him down.'

I felt like grabbing my mother and shaking her silly. '*Mother.* Please. Just tell us the whole story.'

Mother gave me a tight-lipped *nope* look.

'Ves,' said Jay. 'I know this is a highly inappropriate question, but...'

'But?'

'How old are you?'

'Thirty—' I stopped.

'Thirty-one,' said Mother. 'And a bit.'

My mouth felt suddenly dry. 'And how long ago was this wild party you've never forgotten?'

She smiled, very faintly. 'Thirty-two years, or thereabouts.'

There followed one of those pauses people call pregnant. In this case, it was pregnant with an imminent explosion courtesy of me. 'No,' I said, backing away. 'I know my father. His name is Richard Rosser and he's a dragon photographer. Last known location somewhere in Croatia.'

'It probably is Richard,' said Mother.

'*Probably?*'

'I've never been certain. And that's eaten away at me over the years.'

I said a few inarticulate things at considerable volume.

Jay, rather uncharacteristically, came my way and wrapped an arm around my shoulders. 'Calm,' he said. 'Everything will be fine.'

I breathed a bit. Fine. Everything would be fine. 'So I might be the daughter of Richard Rosser, absentee father extraordinaire and who could blame him considering I'm only *probably his daughter,* or my dad might actually be some kind of faerie lyre-player.'

'Yeah. Also,' said Mother.

'Ohgod,' I said.

'I'm not totally sure he isn't King Evelaern.'

If my previous explosion was colourful, the next one was still more interesting. I may have turned purple in the face. Mother even put up her hands to ward me off, like I might have hit her or something. That's how livid I was. (No, of course I didn't hit her).

Jay hung onto me as though I might levitate with pure fury otherwise. 'Ves,' he said, soothingly (he had to say it a few times before it registered with me). 'Ves. He's not King Evelaern. The king's dead, remember? Everyone says so.'

Mother snorted. 'And if *everyone* is saying something then it must be true.'

'There has been *way too much royalty* in my life lately,' I spat, with venom. 'First sodding Baron Alban's a sodding prince, then Torvaston the Second's a runaway absentee monarch with a bad magick habit, and now *I'm a faerie princess?'*

'You probably aren't,' said Mother.

'Probably?!'

'That's what I'd like to find out. Wouldn't you?' She looked blandly at me, with that unshakeable calm of hers that I've always envied. If someone had given my mother this kind of news, she would have thought it over in silence, nodded and said, 'Interesting.'

I tried it. 'Interesting.'

'Isn't it?'

Jay said, 'So this is why you really brought Ves in?'

'Pretty much. Though the fact that she's got those pipes is a highly convenient coincidence. Or then again, what if it isn't?'

'A coincidence?'

'Right. Who'd that unicorn be more likely to give the King's pipes to than his daughter?'

We all looked at the unicorn in question, who was unconcernedly dozing in the sun.

'So you found out that I had those pipes,' I said, more calmly. 'Is that when you started this crazy mission to get back into the Yllanfalen kingdom?'

'Yes.'

'Okay. And why do we need Jay?'

'Hey,' said Jay.

I patted his arm. 'No offence meant. I mean, my execrable parent made rather a point of my bringing our Waymaster along.'

'We need Jay in case your maybe-father's not here,' said Mother. 'It's been decades. I'm hoping he's still somewhere in these parts, but if he's not, we'll need a whirly wizard.'

'Whirly wizard,' Jay repeated. 'I like it.'

Mother flashed him a swift grin. 'Shall we get on, then?' she said, briskly business-like.

I leaned on Jay for a second as every organ I owned sank into my boots. Then I straightened. 'Fine, sure. Let's go and turn the life of one Cordelia Vesper upside down.'

'Mine, too,' said Mother.

'Fun for all the family,' said Jay.

WHEN THE LADY AT the shop said theirs was a musical society, she really wasn't kidding. Finding the lyre-player turned out to be not so much looking for a needle in a haystack as looking for a needle in a needlestack.

We went into every shop we saw, especially those with a musical bent, and asked after lyre musicians. Every single one furnished us with a long list. We asked after the moon-silver lyre, too, only to receive the same news we'd heard before: that lyre is lost. Gone. Missing for years, lost for decades.

Mother began asking about the party that lived so vividly in her memory, and the man who'd played the moonsilver lyre on that night.

Rather a mistake.

'That must have been the Feast of Luirlan,' everybody said — except for those who called it Anhaernyll's Day, or Ellryndon, or something-or-other else. 'Anyone can play the moonsilver lyre at the Feast of Luirlan.'

'But nobody played it like the man I'm looking for,' Mother insisted. 'He was like... like a god.'

She won herself a nice selection of strange looks, but no real information. Not even when attempting to describe him. A tall, graceful man with pale skin and rich brown hair worn on the long side? Dressed in an embroidered tunic, with a blue jewel at his throat? We saw at least half a dozen men fitting that approximate description inside of an hour.

'This is hopeless,' I said at last. 'We could do this all week and get nowhere. Are you sure you don't remember the man's name, Mum?'

'People weren't bothering so much with details, that night.'

'Right.' I mentally brushed aside the images conjured of my mother, deep in dissipation. 'You know, if he was secretly King Evelaern not being as dead as generally supposed, I feel like that's a thing people would notice.'

'There's no one to beat the Faerie at glamour,' said my mother. 'He'd be keeping a low profile.'

'Why?' I retorted. 'Because he got bored with being the ultimate lord of a faerie kingdom?'

'Maybe he did,' said Jay. In response to my look of enquiry, he added, 'Alban doesn't seem to be enjoying the idea very much, does he?'

'You know Prince Alban?' said Mother sharply.

'Recent acquaintance. Anyway—'

My mother gave a long whistle. 'You're on the rise, my girl.'

'You don't know the half of it,' said Jay, grimly.

'Let's shelve that topic for another time, shall we?' I interposed. 'One incredibly complicated personal problem at a time, if you please. Let's get back to maybe-Dad. If we can't find him by description, we'll have to play detective.'

'The lyre,' Jay said.

'Right. We have one missing artefact of improbably enormous power, and at least some reason to think that your erstwhile lover might know something about that. Therefore: if we find out what became of the lyre, maybe we'll find the player, too.'

Mother looked sceptical, but she nodded. 'Which means what?'

'I knew all those Nancy Drew novels would come in handy someday.'

'We're hiring Nancy Drew? Cordelia, you do know she isn't real?'

'We're going to find the lyre through detective work,' I said, shooting Mother Dearest a look of supreme annoyance. '*I'm* Nancy Drew.'

Mother rolled her eyes.

'You can be George.'

'Remind me which adventure featured George losing a hand.'

'Details.'

'Don't tell me I'm Ned.' Jay took a step back.

I felt faintly injured at that. 'You don't have to play with us if you don't want to.' Then my brain caught up with the implications of that sentence. 'Wait. You've read Nancy Drew?'

'Who hasn't?'

I beamed at him, all injury forgotten. 'Forgiven.'

Jay brushed this aside. 'All right, lady sleuth. Where do we start?'

'Hm. Well. Since no one can agree as to when was the last time the lyre was played — and that's hardly surprising if it was many years ago — then maybe we start with the last place it was *known* to occupy.'

'The vault,' said Jay.

'The one which that nice lady at the music shop specifically discouraged us from bothering to enquire about.'

'Significant?'

'Could be. I mean, it seems like the best time to wander off with the lyre would be during one of those feast days, when it's no longer under lock and key. But you heard what all those people said. *Anyone* can play the moonsilver lyre on days like those, and probably a lot did. You don't think that would maybe be a bad time to try to take it? When everyone's waiting their turn to play? If your turn came up and you promptly did a runner with the lyre, I think someone would notice.'

'Fair point,' said Jay. 'So it could have been lifted from the vault after all.'

'Most likely. No one's been saying that a thief took it and ran, they're just saying that it's not in the vault anymore. So, I want to see that vault.'

'Great.' Jay subjected the square we were standing in to a brief, business-like survey. 'Where is it?'

'Really good question.'

8

FAERIE BEING WHAT IT is, the Vault of Promise couldn't be in some mere ordinary location. There's no Central Bank of Goodies in the lands of the Yllanfalen, with lock boxes and safes; there isn't even a secret room somewhere, complete with armed guards and unpronounceable passwords.

No, the Yllanfalen have an island in the middle of a lake. The island in question is called *Lyllora Var*, it's literally about fifty feet across, and it's made out of white rock laced with starry quartz. On this island is a bubble of light, and in that bubble of light is — or was — the moonsilver lyre.

So far, so lovely.

The catch with *Lyllora Var*? It isn't there.

Neither is the lake.

Because this is Faerie, so there's a magic fountain that usually isn't there either. When it is, it's under the old king's palace. When it feels disposed, it is so obliging as to pour forth the waters of this wondrous lake, and when the lake's restored *then* the island appears.

By the time we had got the entire story pieced together, I was no longer surprised that the Yllanfalen seemed so happy to share details of this super-secret vault. I mean, why not? It's not like we were *ever* going to reach it.

'Are we at all inclined to reconsider the idea that someone swiped the lyre from this vault?' I said, as we turned away from our latest interrogee. The woman in question had outright sneered at us. Sneered! I judged we were not the only hopeful treasure-hunters to show up with searching questions about this lyre. She, too, had trotted out the same line about the lyre's being missing.

'No,' said Jay. 'They retrieve the thing every festival, remember? Or did, before it vanished. So it's achievable.'

'Wait,' called the woman upon whom I had just resolutely turned my back.

I turned around.

Her gaze, though, was not fixed upon me. She was looking at Addie, who had wandered off for a large part of the afternoon, and had now wandered back. 'That unicorn,' she said. 'Where did you...?'

Having grown tired of the sneering lady already, I merely waved my pipes by way of response.

'Let me see those,' she snapped.

'No—' I began.

'Ves,' Jay said, apparently having anticipated this response. 'She may have something useful to tell us.'

I handed them over with great reluctance, and stood vigilant, in case she should make a break for the hills with my pipes in hand.

She did not, however. She inspected them most closely, her young face intent, and ran her fingers several times over the silver. Then she put them to her lips, and played a ditty of a tune I'd never heard before.

My lovely Adeline paused in the act of nibbling grass by the roadside, and lifted her head. She stared at the woman who'd moved in on my perfect pipes, and the woman, damn her, stared back.

If I was expecting some explanation as to what that was all about, I was out of luck. The woman merely handed my pipes back to me, her face unreadable, and said: 'Why are you interested in the moonsilver lyre?'

'We're from the Society for the Preservation of Magickal Heritage,' I rattled off, feeling obscurely annoyed. 'It's our job to research ancient artefacts.'

'Research?' she said. 'Why this one?'

'It's also our job to rescue ancient artefacts,' said Jay.

'So you came to "rescue" the lyre,' she said, her mouth curving satirically. 'Did you know it was missing before you arrived?'

'It's my fault,' said Mother. 'I brought them here. I've seen the lyre before, you see, and I wanted to see it again.'

'Why?'

'Research.'

The woman looked from me to Jay to Mother, exasperated. 'Do you even have any idea what you are trying to accomplish?'

'Nope,' I muttered.

Jay elbowed me. 'Look, we'd like to get the lyre back for you,' he said. 'It's our job. We're hoping to begin at the vault, find out what happened there.'

He received a strange look in response. 'What if it does not wish to return?'

'Wish?' faltered Jay. 'It has wishes?'

'It has... a destiny,' she said, spectacularly unhelpful. 'The same as you or I.'

'Was its destiny to be purloined by a thief?'

'Is that what happened?' Her head tilted.

'I don't know,' said Jay flatly. 'Is it?'

The woman looked dreamily up at the sky, probably preparing another fatuously mystical statement for our benefit.

'For goodness' sake,' I said. 'By my unicorn's silky nose hairs, will you help us or not?'

'Very well,' she said. 'For the sake of Ylariane, and those pipes.'

'Who or what is Ylariane?'

Adeline whickered, and bumped my elbow with her nose.

'...Oh.'

The woman's sardonic smile was back. 'I will need your sworn word,' she said, gravely. 'If you find the lyre, you will return it to the Yllanfalen.'

'Of course,' I said. 'The Society always repatriates artefacts, wherever possible.'

'Very good. You will be held to that.' There was a shiver of something in her voice as she spoke, something rather dark. It occurred to me that, however obliging the Yllanfalen appeared to be about answering our questions (for the most part), they would not be easy to fool, or to betray.

Fortunately, we had no plans to do either. Did we? I eyed my mother with momentary misgivings, for she was wearing an expression of mild congeniality which seemed at odds with her character.

I'd have to keep a close eye on her.

We had interrupted the Yllanfalen woman in the middle of shopping, I'd judged from the quantity of small parcels tucked into a willow basket she carried. She now lifted the basket as though placing it onto a shelf — whereupon it disappeared. Then she turned to us with a nod, dusted off her hands, and said: 'We'll be needing a few of Ylariane's friends, I imagine?'

'You are going with us?' said Mother.

'Did you want a guide to the lake, or not?' answered the woman with faint irritation.

Mother held up her hands. 'Actually, we do.'

'Then first we must return to the palace. The unicorns?'

I hurried to obey, whistling Addie's bouquet of tunes upon my pipes. She stamped one silvery hoof, and spat out grass. 'How did you do that?' I blurted, when I'd finished.

Our guide's head tilted again. 'What?'

'The way you stored your basket! I've never seen it done.'

'It is an old trick, among the Yllanfalen.'

'So how do you do it?'

She gave another of her faint smiles. 'If you find and return the lyre, I will give you the spell. Is that fair?'

Privately, I wasn't sure such a spell (however handy) was quite a fair trade for an ancient lyre of unimaginable power and priceless value, but since we weren't here to steal the thing anyway, it seemed a solid prize. I agreed.

'What's your name?' I said after, with a smile. I might have been regretting my earlier irritation with her. After all, she was Faerie. A certain ethereal mysticism was natural to her, in the same way that drinking, vulgarity and a love of sports are natural to humankind. I shouldn't really hold her fey qualities against her.

'I am called Ayllindariorana,' she said.

'That's... not going to happen.'

She glanced at me, and as the friends of Adeline/Ylariane came galloping up the street to aid us, I detected a gleam of mischief in her sea-blue eyes. 'You can call me Ayllin.'

'Better.'

AND SO, BACK TO King Evelaern's Halls. We galloped through a shroud of hazy, ethereal mist clinging to its pale, perfect walls, and its slender spires twinkled with magick under the afternoon sun.

Odd of the Yllanfalen, I thought. All this astonishing beauty and glory, and they treated it as a party pad.

I'd seen no sign of an entrance as we rode up to the imposing palace, but Ayllin led us away from the splendid frontage and around the side. There, hidden between two slim pilasters, was a tall, narrow door.

Or, it would have been were it not filled in with white bricks.

Ayllin retrieved a set of syrinx pipes of her own, a pair that looked wrought from quartz. Her song echoed upon the air, a mere handful of notes that rang out clear and sharp. As the sounds died away, the slender arch shimmered and became a door of white oak wood.

'Thank you,' said Ayllin gravely, and the door swung slowly open.

In we went.

'Who were you thanking?' I asked as we filed into a spacious antechamber, cool and dim, its walls all twined about with pale-leaved vines.

'The sprites,' she said. 'They do not often show themselves.'

'They're the keepers of the doors?'

'Among other things.'

I remembered the woman in the music shop. She'd sold me a garden song, on the grounds that the sprites liked it. I tucked these bits of information away. If sprites grew gardens and kept doors for the Yllanfalen, what else might they do? What might they know?

I also did my best to commit Ayllin's door-opening sprite-song to memory.

Ayllin paused in the midst of the chamber, and smiled at the parade of unicorns that had followed us inside. 'You do not wish to trail after us all the way to the lake,' she told them. 'There are stairs.'

The night-black stallion, for whom I knew no name, stamped one hoof, and shook his great head.

'There is grass outside,' I offered, without much hope. Addie's greedy heart beat only for chips. Her friends probably had unusual tastes, too.

Still, Mr. Midnight turned and ambled away again, followed by a goldish-coloured mare and a creature the colour of raspberry meringue. Addie stood her ground.

I hugged her around her velvety-soft neck. 'Love you for your loyalty, but you should go too. Enjoy the sun. Chips coming later.'

Addie shook out her mane, lipped at my sleeve, and finally went away. Did I imagine that flick of the tail in Ayllin's direction as she strutted past? Was it really as dismissive as it looked?

It occurred to me that my faithful friend did not quite trust Ayllin, and I wondered why.

The lady in question had not waited to witness the departure of the unicorns. She was already halfway across the room, walking purposefully, my mother in hot pursuit. There was a similarity in their no-nonsense stride, I noticed with interest.

Jay beckoned. 'Come on. She'll be fine.'

'Oh, I know. She's made of concrete, diamonds and solid steel. Nothing can touch her.'

'Sort of like you, then?'

I blinked. 'No. Well, maybe the diamonds part. I wouldn't mind that.'

'They do sparkle,' Jay agreed.

'Gloriously.' We followed Ayllin and Mother to the far side of the room, down a spacious passage beyond, and then Ayllin started down a wide staircase of polished, if dusty, wood.

Only then did I recall a detail that had glided past me before.

The lake was *under* the palace, and we were rapidly descending underground.

'I feel you should know,' I called, hastening to catch up. 'There are—'

'*Lindworms*,' growled my mother. 'I'm telling you.'

'They won't come this far,' said Ayllin airily, her pace not slowing one whit.

A feral roar shook the stonework, attended by a great, deep rumbling in the walls and floor.

'I—' began Ayllin, and faltered. 'How did it get so—!'

She got no further, for an enormous lindworm burst into view, scales glittering darkly over its sleek wyrm hide, jaws agape. Ayllin gave a shriek — and disappeared in a cloud of dust, earth and lindworm.

9

'GODS *CURSE IT*,' I swore, groping for my pipes and my wand. I should have been better prepared, but it had happened so damned fast — Ayllin hadn't even reached the bottom of the staircase.

'Pipes,' barked my mother to me.

'Ayllin—'

'*Pipes.* Your job is to ruin that damned lindworm.'

I don't know what Mother planned to do, but Jay had his rubescent Wand in hand and was running for the stairs. My mother was going to extract Ayllin with her bare hands, apparently — or hand, anyway.

Me, though. Ruin. Right.

This time when I played, I went for a different song. The last one was a lullaby; my only goal had been to keep the thing pacified long enough for us to escape. Lindworms aren't up there on the same level of rarity as, say, griffins, but we don't wreck them without good cause either.

Considering the state of my mother's dead companions, her missing hand, and now the probable state of our guide, I figured Mum was right. This was good cause.

I blew a swift, sharp blast on my pretty pipes, and the sound split the air with the intensity of a thunderclap. I repeated the sound, twice — thrice. The lindworm was a mass of roiling, scaled flesh by that time, with poor Ayllin wound up somewhere within its muscular coils. The second wave of sound sent a tearing shudder through its miserable carcass. The third brought it to a temporary, shuddering halt.

At the fourth, there was blood.

I went after it, blazing fury, my song growing more intense and more discordant with each shrieking note I played. I *forced* the damned thing into submission, alternating blasts of my pipes with waves of layered curses shot from the tip of my lovely Sunstone Wand.

By the time I was finished, the lindworm lay insensate, its massive body filling the passage below from floor to ceiling. Blood had leaked from its eyes, its mouth, what passed for its ears, and run all over the stairs. Its jaws hung slack, revealing rows of shark-teeth that would never chew anybody to bits again.

'That's for my mother's gods-damned *hand!*' I shrieked at it, and kicked it.

Ayllin, mercifully, was alive, though bathed in such a quantity of blood that I feared it couldn't be for long. Once again, I wished fervently for Rob, and cursed my mother's secretiveness. I ran over to Jay and my mother, who were supporting Ayllin between them. I think I hadn't imagined the moment, mid-battle, where Ayllin had popped free of the lindworm's coils and gone sailing into the air, only to float down in a flurry of feathers.

'Will she live?' I gasped.

'Most of the blood isn't hers,' said Mother tersely, checking Ayllin over with a remarkably professional air for someone with zero knowledge of medicine. 'Lindworm's,' she added unnecessarily.

Ayllin groaned, and shook herself. She looked more dazed than destroyed, to my relief — but also to my surprise. The worm had hit her with the force of a train. 'Borrow— your — pipes?' she panted, looking at me.

This time, I handed them over promptly.

She began a lilting song much better suited to their airy, faerie delicacy than the Song of Ruin I'd been playing a moment before. I felt cocooned in sound, and, gradually, refreshed; it was like being wrapped in a warm blanket on a cold winter day, and pumped full of hot chocolate.

Ayllin began to look revived.

Immediate alarm over Ayllin passed, I was at leisure to notice Jay.

'What?' I said.

He blinked his wide, wide eyes, and went on staring at me in... horror? Awe? 'What the bloody hell did you do to that worm?'

'Ruined it.'

'I see that.'

I shrugged. 'Had to.'

'Did I know you could do that?'

'You know when Rob said I could handle myself in a fight?'

'No, but okay.'

'Well, he did, and that's what he meant. I just don't *like* to do it.'

'It's Rob's job.'

'That it is, and he's better at it by an order of magnitude.'

'That scares the living daylights out of me.'

'It should. You never want to get on Rob's bad side.'

Mother spoke up. 'Rob Foster's still with the Society, is he?'

That got my attention. 'You know Milady *and* Rob?'

'I've been alive for a while.'

'So what? Rob's the quiet type, and Milady never leaves Home.'

Mum raised a brow. 'Doesn't she?'

Jay and I maintained identically stunned silences for about four seconds.

'Er,' said Jay.

'What?' said I.

Mother gave her secretive smile, and I rolled my eyes.

'She's just messing with us,' I told Jay. 'She does that.'

Mum nodded and turned back to Ayllin. 'That must be it.'

And, curse her, she left a note of doubt growing in my mind.

'Right,' I said. '*Anyway.* On with the larceny show?'

Ayllin looked sharply at me, and I coughed.

'On with the detecting show, I meant. It just feels like larceny, what with all the fighting-past-lindworm-guardians and breaking-into-ancient-vaults...'

'It is starting to feel remarkably like a heist,' Jay agreed.

I played a few notes from the theme to Ocean's Eight.

'Stop it,' said Mother.

I sighed, and trailed up to the felled lindworm. Thankfully, it had stopped twitching. 'Next problem,' I said, trying futilely to see past the creature. Its enormous body blocked the entire passage, both ways. 'How do we get past this thing?'

'Can't you, I don't know, liquify it or something?' Jay made hand-waving-magick-casting gestures, as though that might help.

'No,' I said. 'Can you?'

'I'm just the new guy.'

'With Waymastery powers to die for, an odd talent for fae music he still thinks is a secret, and with gods-know-what other skills shoved up his black leather sleeves — but just the new guy.'

'She's too perceptive,' said Jay to my mother.

'Annoying, isn't it?' said she.

Jay grinned at me. 'The thing about being a Waymaster is, nobody ever wants to talk about anything else.'

'So are you hiding any talents that might vaporise a lindworm?'

'Still nope.'

'Damnit.'

'I might be able to open a door in it, though.'

'Open a— *in it*? What?'

'It's a kind of warped sidespell of Waymastery.'

'No it isn't,' said Mother flatly. 'If you mean what I think you mean, that's advanced stuff. Do you think just anybody can open a damned void in a fresh corpse?'

'True,' said Jay. 'But it occurs more commonly in Waymasters. Nobody knows why.'

'Jay,' I said. 'Whatever Milady's paying you, it's nowhere near enough.'

Jay glanced meaningfully at the destroyed lindworm. 'I'd say the same of you.'

'And now you're starting to scare me too.'

'I can't do it on anything that's alive,' Jay said quickly. But then, to my horror, he paused. 'Well. I don't know for certain that I can't, as I've never tried. If I did, the Ministry would sign an immediate warrant for my capture and execution, and I'd turn myself in gladly.'

'Let's get on with it,' Ayllin cut in.

She had a point. The day was wearing on. I stepped back out of Jay's way — I didn't want to be too near him while he was boring holes in organic matter.

He did some things. Don't ask me what, I cannot even begin to comprehend what was going on with him.

But when he'd finished, a neat circular hole had appeared, running right through the centre of the lindworm's body. It was just about tall enough for us to pass through, if we stooped.

Its edges were so perfect, it could've been bored by a machine.

'Hang on,' I said, as Mother made to stride straight on. I lit up a fireball and sent it through.

The plan was to light up the other side, so we could see if any other lindworms were lying in wait. But my fireball sputtered and died before it had passed more than halfway through the lindworm.

'It's a patch of nothing,' Jay reminded me. 'No air.'

'Right. We do it the exciting way, then.' I went in, trying not to think about why my feet squelched as I walked through Jay's void-door. I lit up another fireball the moment I reached the cold corridor beyond, and let it shine brightly.

The corridor was reassuringly empty.

'We're good,' I called. 'Onward.'

Ayllin marched past me, swiftly followed by Mother. Jay and I brought up the rear. I felt a moment's concern for Ayllin out there in front, again — what if there was more than one lindworm down here? But, the woman appeared to be indestructible. Whatever she was doing to protect herself was clearly effective. I was getting curious about Yllanfalen magick.

The King's Halls were rather better supplied with cellars and under-passages than I'd imagined, for we went down and down into the bowels of the building, and it got steadily colder and darker. Not that this had much of an effect on the stunning beauty of the place. When it's Yllanfalen, it's not the frigid, miserable chill of early February, with not a scrap of warmth or joy looming on the horizon; it's the glittering cold of snowflakes and clear ice, a darkness that's velvet and enchanting rather than gloomy.

'I'd really like to talk to your interior designers,' I said to Ayllin, as we marched through some kind of subterranean ballroom draped in cobwebs — the attractive, misty kind, of course — and hung with exquisite silks.

'Can't,' she said tersely.

'Not all of them, certainly. All this must be the work of hundreds—'

'Zero,' said Ayllin.

'I beg your pardon?'

'None of this,' and she waved a hand, somewhat impatiently, at a rose-marble fountain in miniature singing airily to itself as it poured icy water into the air, 'was built by either mortal hand or faerie.'

'Then by whose?'

She shrugged. 'By magick. The Halls develop as they will. Though, they have ceased to grow at the rate they once did. I believe only two new rooms have manifested in the past twenty years.'

Manifested? 'Giddy gods, you mean to say all this just *appears?*'

'It isn't that simple. Though at the same time, it is.'

'Could you maybe just explain?'

'If I could, I... well, I might.' I heard that mischievous flash of a smile again in her voice. 'It is a process that is not fully understood. The prevailing theory is that it is the product of the dreams of the Yllanfalen, that the Halls respond to our collective ideas, needs and wishes.'

'If this is what the inside of an Yllanfalen head looks like...' I began to reconsider my ideas about my possible parentage, for who wouldn't want to generate such ethereal beauty with a thought? Then again, this must be an argument for my being one hundred percent human. The inside of *my* head looked like... a cluttered yard, with books, teapots and pancakes piled willy-nilly about, too many colours crammed into a small space (some of them clashing), and a litter of half-finished notions and abandoned dreams coating everything like dust.

'I don't know how you find your way through it,' growled Mother. 'Last time I was here, I was lost within two minutes. But, that was part of the fun at the time.'

'Most of it is ancient,' said Ayllin. 'Hush, now. We draw near the fountain.'

We'd drawn near to, and passed, about eight fountains already; I gathered that the fountain held some kind of special significance in the collective consciousness of the Yllanfalen, if this was indeed the manifestation of their dreams. Since every one of those fountains had been utterly exquisite, I had high hopes for the important one.

They were not disappointed.

We fetched up before an enormous stone door, its surface deeply etched with runic characters all filled in with quartz. I couldn't read them; I didn't even recognise the language. The door had an inflexible air I found most unpromising, for by the looks of it, we'd as easily persuade a mountain to step aside.

But Ayllin said something incomprehensible in a voice that rang with a faint melody, and the bejewelled runes lit up with white fire.

The door creaked ponderously open.

10

WHAT LAY ON THE other side was not a room at all, but an expansive cave. Whether this, too, was some kind of magickal manifestation created by the Yllanfalen, or whether it had always been there, I had no way to determine. If the latter, it had been co-opted into service as some kind of sacred site, by the looks of it, for it had a hushed, hallowed air. Stone worn smooth by time stretched before us, the ground sloping gently into the centre. The walls of the cavern swooped up into a kind of natural vaulted ceiling, far over our heads. They were empty of things one might expect to see in a cave system, like stalagmites and stalactites. Instead, they bore extensive carvings depicting scenes of Yllanfalen life. Many featured an unusually tall fellow with a crown, a lyre in hand, and pipes hanging around his neck, so, no prizes for guessing who was revered here.

They liked their jewels, the Yllanfalen. Quartz and beryl and spinel and a hundred other gems adorned everything, and I could see that because they were all lit up with the same clear fire that had emblazoned the portal through which we'd entered (I'm giving up terming it merely a door. No word but *portal* could befit such absurd— I mean, such wondrous grandeur).

The fountain occupied the central position in the middle, where the ground arrived at its lowest point. It rose to the height of three Baron-Albans, composed of five tiers, and as far as I could tell from this distance it was made out of clear glass radiating moonlight. Lovely.

All the cavern around it would fill up with water, I supposed, to form that mythical lake we were looking for. Which presented one immediate problem: if we managed to switch on the Magick Fountain of Dreams, how were we to avoid promptly drowning in the Faerie Lake of Bespelled Waters?

One problem at a time, Ves, hm?

My wonderfully prosaic mother stood taking in all this magickal magnificence with an expression profoundly unimpressed. 'Right,' she said. 'And how do we persuade that frippery thing to start spewing water?'

Ayllin looked pained at my mother's soulless choice of words, as well she might. She made no answer, however. Instead she took up her own syrinx pipes and began to play a tune I can only term ethereal. The melody echoed around the cavern, swelling in volume and richness with every note. That softly-glimmering moonlight centred upon the fountain grew stronger, and clear water began to pour from its spout.

The melody was not a complicated one; I soon had its measure. I joined in, playing a low counterpart, and to my surprise the water flow promptly tripled. The skysilver really did give these things a bit more *oomph*, huh?

The fountain might be pumping away merrily, but it still seemed to me that the wide cavern would take weeks to fill. Soon, though, water was lapping at our toes, and then we were soaked to our ankles. 'Er,' said Jay. 'Got a boat, or something?'

No sooner had he spoken than a boat appeared, drifting up to us with the serenity of a construct whose existence is in no way impossible. Never mind that it, too, appeared to be made of glass, and it shone with the same pale moonglow as the fountain. It had one of those fanciful swan's head arrangements, too, and a slender set of oars. I eyed it with misgiving, but Jay got straight in and picked up the oars. Since he didn't disappear through the bottom of the boat, I followed suit. As did Mother.

Ayllin, though, did not. She had levitated herself — standing, incomprehensibly, on some kind of a giant silvery leaf, and where had that come from, hm? Is the entirety of Yllanfalen made out of magick or something? She did not cease to play, even as her leaf rose smoothly to the ceiling, taking her with it.

My mother looked as though she'd like to take the boat's pretty oars off Jay, but remembered her missing hand with chagrin. She sat scowling at him instead. 'Don't tickle the water. Row!'

'To where?' protested Jay, most reasonably.

But Mother lifted an arm — the one without the hand — and pointed her stump imperiously at the centre of the lake. The water had risen high enough now to engulf the fountain, as tall as it was, and a thick mist had collected where it once stood. Through the silvery-white fog I could just make out the outlines of a tiny spit of land.

The island-vault had checked in.

Jay rowed. The lake was not all that large, and there were no currents to fight with; we made rapid progress, and soon drew near to the island. I had time enough to note, with fascination, that the waters were full of lithe fish with twilight-blue scales, and that the bottom had developed a vibrant crop of pond weed, lake mosses and other vegetation — and then Jay had the boat up against the island and had jumped out. He stood holding a hand in my mother's direction, but I could have told him that was a waste of time. She made a point of reaching the bank unaided, earning herself a sardonic flicker of Jay's brow.

I accepted his help with gratitude, largely because it is quite tricky to navigate such a manoeuvre while also playing the syrinx pipes. Once my feet hit solid, quartzy ground, however, Ayllin ceased to play, so I let my song die away too. The sudden silence echoed.

'*Lyllora Var* welcomes you,' she said mysteriously, with a smile I did not much like. It had too much smug mischief in it.

'How nice,' said mother, folding her arms. She stared coolly at Ayllin. 'You're keeping a comfy distance, I note.'

Ayllin's only response was a graceful wave, like a queen, and then she stepped off her leaf and — disappeared.

'Do they have some kind of magick school here?' I breathed. 'I'd enrol like a shot.'

'More importantly,' said Jay. 'We appear to be stranded.'

He was right. The boat had dematerialised as thoroughly as Ayllin, and the door through which we had entered must now lie several feet under water.

Mother snickered. 'She got rid of us very neatly.'

She had, at that. If I had wondered at any point why she was so helpful, when the rest of Yllanfalen had been broadly evasive, here was my answer.

'Well,' I said, turning my back to the problem of the disappearing boat and the submerged door. 'Let's get what we came for. Then we can worry about how to get out.'

'Right.' Jay joined me. The swirling mists were so pervasive, they cloaked almost every inch of the island in an opaque shroud we could scarcely see through. It was pretty mist, I noted, like everything else in this absurd place: it shone as though under moonlight, and there were traces of something that glittered.

The ground was uneven and very hard. It, too, sparkled, so I observed that Ayllin had not exaggerated when she'd said the place was made out of quartz-rock. Nothing much seemed to be growing on it, save an occasional, blithely impossible patch of velvety moss. I linked arms with Jay on my left and Mother on my right, unwilling to lose either of them in the fog, and we walked slowly forward. The lights I'd sent up with a flick of my Wand did not help much, but at least they could prevent us from walking into anything.

Not that there proved to be anything to walk into. We walked from one side of the island to the other in the space of a few minutes, and encountered nothing at all.

'There was something about a bubble of ligh—' I began, and suddenly I saw it: a bubble indeed, pearly with moonglow, and floating about eight feet over our heads.

It was empty.

'So the lyre's really gone,' Mother mused.

'You thought they might be lying?' I asked.

'Yes. We got the same story from too many people, and promptly, too. Very consistent. Very like a collective lie.'

'Why would they lie about its absence?'

'To protect it from treasure-hunters like us,' said Mother with her wolfish grin.

'Fair,' I said. 'You might still be right. Ayllin's cordially conducting us down here only to leave us stranded seems rather to support the idea.'

'A decoy vault?' said Jay. 'A complicated solution, but I like it.'

'It might explain why everything's so sodding elaborate,' I muttered.

'Enough theorising,' said Mother crisply. 'Time for some facts.' And, to my puzzlement, she sat cross-legged upon the ground where she stood and laid her hands — er, *hand* — against the rocky ground.

Nobody spoke for a bit.

'Mum,' I said after a while. 'What are you doing?'

She'd shut her eyes, but now they snapped open again. 'What do you think I'm doing?'

'No idea.'

She blinked. 'Really?'

'Really.'

Her frown appeared. 'I'm looking for traces of past magick performed here.'

'You can do that?' I was startled. It wasn't so much that it was a rare ability, as that few people thought it worth the trouble of developing it. The Hidden Ministry had a team of magickal forensics experts, if you will, attached to their Forbidden Magicks department; other than that, it was mostly popular with archaeolo—

'Why do you think I became an archaeologist?' Mother said, forestalling my thought. 'It's my best talent.'

'I hadn't thought about it.'

'We've discussed this before.'

'No,' I said steadily. 'We haven't.'

The frown deepened. 'Are you sure?'

'Mum. We pretty much haven't discussed anything before.'

She had no response to make to that, apparently, for her eyes shut again and she fell silent.

Jay and I waited, he trying not to signal a thousand disapproving thoughts with his eyes, and largely failing. At least they were directed at Mother this time, rather than me.

'Right,' said Mother after a while. 'It's trickier than usual down here, because the whole damned place is soaked in magick. Everything we're sitting on is the product of it. But there are traces of something that feels like music-magick still lingering here. Rather faded. Probably from at least a couple of decades ago. Might be the lyre? And there's something else, too, something much bigger.'

'Bigger?' I prompted.

'More powerful. And unusual. I'd say it's a spell that was cast only the *once*, also some time ago, but it's left a stronger residue for all that.'

'And what was it?'

'I think someone opened some kind of a gate.' She stood up, dusting off her hand on her ragged trousers. 'Much like the one we came through.'

'You mean...' I thought for a second. 'You mean back into Britain proper?'

'Most likely, yes.'

See, magickal gates aren't exactly portals. They don't transport you over large distances. They're just doors that lead from regular Britain into the hidden magickal pockets like the Dells and Troll Enclaves — and, of course, the kingdoms of Yllanfalen.

However ordinary that makes them, however, it's no easy matter to open one. No easy matter at all.

'That sounds like the work of a thief, doesn't it?' said Jay. 'Got down here somehow, snatched the lyre, and escaped into Britain with it.'

'Could be,' said Mother. 'Though it isn't so easy to open such a gate as all that.'

And that's the truth. If it were easy, we'd spend a lot less time searching for existing gates when we wanted to cross realms. But this *was* an existing gate, near enough. 'Next question,' said I. 'How far faded is it? Could it be revived?'

Mum looked at me. 'You want to follow?'

'Why not? We need a way out anyway.'

She nodded. 'Let's see what we can do.'

11

MUM WAS LOOKING AT Jay. 'That trick with the nothing-ness. You said you'd open a door *through* the lindworm.'

'Not the same kind of door. I was just trying to express the general concept in comprehensible language.'

'All right. But could it be adapted for this gate?'

Jay took a moment to consider. 'No,' he finally said. 'A gate — the kind you mean — is an insubstantial thing, it has no tangible presence. In a sense it's already nothing, and I can't open a nothing in nothing.'

Mother took this philosophically, and lapsed into thought.

I wracked my brains, too. What was known about these intra-realm gates? It was the province of the various mag-ickal authorities to maintain existing gate networks; The Hidden Ministry poured a lot of resources into it. And, naturally, they had all kinds of rules about how many gates should remain open, and which should be barred. The Society had no one with those skills, because it wasn't part of our mandate.

That meant I, too, was rather more ignorant about the process than I liked. Opening a new gate is the kind of impossible even I won't venture upon, so I've never considered the matter before.

Course, I told myself, we weren't opening a new gate here. Just freshening up an old one, and purely for the purposes of detective work.

'Ves,' said Mother tightly. She was making strange gestures with her surviving hand, as though she was pulling on an invisible thread. 'Help me here.'

'How?'

'Remember when I taught you to knit?'

'You never taught me to knit.'

'I did, when you were six. You were almost as bad at it as I was.'

'How is this relevant?'

'Well.' She was sweating now, her face glistening in the moonlight. 'If you think of the magickal world as a thing knitted up out of — of — well, *magick,* then it can also be unknitted. Someone's gone through a door here, and they may have firmly closed it behind themselves, but *the door's still here.*'

'You're unravelling it?'

'So to speak. Here.' She grabbed my hand and thrust it out before herself. And I felt something. Nothing tangible; more like a sensation that shivered through my skin, neither heat nor cold but something beyond those two things. Whatever it was wound around my hand like — ugh, like I'd thrust my arm into a knot of spider's webs. 'You feel that?'

'I wish a bit that I didn't, but yes.'

'Great. Grab a handful and pull.'

I obeyed — but the moment Mum let go of my hand, the sensations vanished and I was groping at empty air. 'You've a sensitivity I lack, Mum. You'll need to guide me.'

'Fine. I'll do this, you do that.'

We did all that, Mum keeping a firm grip on my wrist with her healthy hand and me using both of mine to tear holes in the magickal fabric of the Halls of Yllanfalen. As mother/daughter bonding events go, it was a weird one, but I'd take it over nothing at all, any day.

After twenty minutes or so, Mum — who'd been periodically waving her stump of an arm about, apparently testing the tear we were making — said, 'Stop. I think we can go through.'

I was happy to obey, for I was trembling with weariness by then. You wouldn't think unravelling the very fabric of magick would take so much out of a person.

'Just need a second,' I gasped.

Mum rolled her eyes and stood up, which was humbling. The woman had lost three friends, a hand and a lot of blood in recent days, and she was still unstoppable.

I hastily pulled myself together.

'You okay?' said Jay, looking at me with a concern I both welcomed and mildly resented.

'Fine,' I said crisply, only belatedly aware of how much I'd sounded like my mother.

The thought crossed Jay's mind too, for his lips twitched.

Mother said, 'We're wasting time,' and promptly hurled herself head-first into nothingness. I tensed, half expecting her to land painfully on the quartz-rock ground, but she disappeared.

I smiled at Jay. 'After me,' I said, and leapt after Mother.

I'd expected to end up on some distant street in Britain somewhere, or perhaps a forgotten heath or moor in the wilder parts of the country.

That's not what happened.

'This,' I said, picking myself up off the floor, 'is not Britain.'

'You don't say,' muttered mother.

We'd emerged at the top of a low, sloping hill ringed all around with pine and conifer trees. The surrounding forest had an air of utter impenetrability, and was shrouded in gloom.

How did I know it was not Britain? Because the same silvery mist that cloaked *Lyllora Var* poured out of those trees, and clung to the base of the hill. Said hill was grown all over with a grasses and moss of a tawny gold colour, and scattered with jewel-like flowers.

At the summit, about three feet away from where we were standing, was a low stone bier upon which lay a corpse.

It was, as one would expect from the Yllanfalen, a most attractive corpse. The man was clearly fae, as improbably beautiful as the rest of his kind, with pale golden hair and a face that looked sculpted from marble. He wore a long robe of the finest silk I've ever seen, richly embroidered, and a delicate golden crown encircled his brow.

Around his neck hung a set of syrinx pipes that looked exactly like mine.

'Found us a king,' I observed.

Jay stood frowning down at the exquisite corpse. 'I don't understand. Why would anyone rip open a gate between the lyre-vault and the king's tomb?'

'I think this is the vault,' said Mother. 'That bubble back there was the gate.'

'But there's nothing here of value, except those pipes.'

'Thief on the loose, remember?'

'Then why not take the pipes, too? If they're as similar to Ves's as they look, that's a Great Treasure just lying there unclaimed.'

'Okay. Let's try it.' I reached for the pipes, and instantly a great bell tolled somewhere, at a volume that left my ears ringing. The ground shook beneath our feet, and thunder cracked the sky.

'Ow,' I said, and speedily withdrew my hand.

'All right, that answers that,' said Jay. 'But then, how was the lyre taken? Was it here at all?'

'I'd say yes,' Mother replied after a moment. 'There are traces of something that seems consistent with a musical Great Treasure. But, I thought that about *Lyllora Var*, too.'

'Who could take it?' I said.

They both looked at me with identical puzzled frowns. 'What?' said Mother.

'Who could physically reach in and take the lyre, if it was once here? Who is that scary thief-repelling enchantment *not* protecting the lyre against?'

'If you've got some idea, Cordelia, please just share it.'

'The lyre belongs to the king, doesn't it?'

'Are we back with the idea that the king isn't dead, because—' Mother stopped, and abruptly bent over the king's gorgeous corpse, her nose inches from his chin. Silence stretched. Then she said: 'I was about to say you were crazy, but maybe not. There are about eighty layers of magick shrouding His Majesty here, and since he's demonstrably not skeletal I might reasonably take them for enchantments of preservation, reverence and so on. But they don't feel quite right. It's something else.'

'Like what?' said I.

She grinned suddenly. 'Ever heard of a faerie stock?'

'You mean the doll type things some of the fae used to leave in the place of stolen human children?'

'That's it, though they're a lot more realistic than a typical doll. Significantly, they do a terrific job of looking like a recently expired person.'

'So,' said Jay. 'These aren't preservation spells, because this man was never alive?'

'I'm thinking so. Which doesn't mean the real king is still alive; he's just as likely to be taking up ground-space as a skeleton somewhere. This is some kind of... shrine to his memory.'

'So it probably included the lyre,' said Jay.

'If the King's pipes are here, it would've made sense to put the lyre here too,' Mother allowed.

'Did the king have any children?' said I. 'Surely the role of monarch would go to one of them when he died. They could've taken the lyre.'

'But not the pipes,' said Jay.

'You're really harping on that point.'

'Because it's a detail that makes no sense. I don't think the thief hypothesis is working too well.'

My dreams of being involved in a daring heist story evaporated. Jay was right.

'Unless,' said Mother, 'whoever took the lyre had a specific use for that one instrument only.'

'Such as?' Jay said. 'I can't recall that anyone's ever said what the thing does, except get passed around at parties.'

'That may prove a crucial question,' said Mother.

'Mum, how about you do your magick-tracing trick so we can get out of here,' I said. 'His Majesty here is giving me the creeps.' Perhaps because (real corpse or not) he looked like he'd died about twelve seconds ago. Just lain down on his personal bier and... died.

'Right.' Mother wandered off, her steps describing a wide circle around his dead-but-not-decaying majesty's bier.

On a whim, I picked up my pipes and played Addie's song.

She appeared so promptly, she cannot have been far away. Up she trotted, unusually lively, shaking her head and whinnying loudly.

'Ves,' said Jay. 'Look. That song's—'

'Done something? I see it.' A pearly light shimmered around the dead king, or his effigy, and I half expected him to wake up.

He did not. Addie, though, went wild. She trotted around the bier, stamping her hooves, and nudging the body with her nose so hard she almost threw the king onto the floor.

Then she picked up her silvery feet and charged away down the hill, mane and tail flying in the winds that blew up out of nowhere.

Jay and I watched this display in wide-eyed silence.

'Follow that unicorn,' said I, and began to run.

'Follow—?' said Jay. 'Can you keep up with a unicorn at full gallop, because I—'

The rest of his sentence was lost to the winds, as I ran full tilt away from him in the direction Adeline had gone. Down and down the hill we went, my feet thudding in the grass, fey winds tossing my hair. There was music in that wind, faint strains but half-heard, but they lent me speed and energy and I could almost have danced my way down the hill.

Adeline still left me far behind, but I ran on, breath turning short as I neared the bottom of the hill and the edge of the dense, dark forest that surrounded it.

Ahead of me, Adeline plunged heedlessly into the trees, her bright, moon-pale coat swallowed up instantly in shadow.

I paused for a moment on the edge of that forest, attempting without success to peer into the gloom.

'Seriously?' panted Jay, drawing up beside me. 'We're going to follow a unicorn into the dark depths of a faerie forest? Did you learn nothing from your bedtime stories as a child?'

'I learned that adventure lies beyond the borders of the familiar.'

'We're way beyond the borders of the familiar already. Does it *have* to be a dark forest, Ves?'

'I'm trusting Addie.'

'She's literally a magickal faerie creature.'

'Haven't you heard?' I grinned, with a shade of my mother's wolfish smile about it. 'So am I. Where's Mum?'

'Here,' growled my mother. 'Don't be a fool, Cordelia.'

'Whyever not? It's been working well for me for the past thirty-one years.'

Mother was limping. The pelting run down the hill hadn't been good for her. 'Why don't you stay here?' I added. 'I'll be right back.'

Without waiting for further arguments, I plunged into the trees, conscious that Addie drew farther away with every minute's delay.

I'll never admit it to my mother, or to Jay, but I instantly regretted it. Three steps was all it took; the trees closed in around me, cutting off most of the light, the temperature dropped by at least ten degrees, and even sounds faded to a muffled distance. I felt cut off from the world, and utterly alone.

'Right,' I said stoutly, and took another step. 'This had better be worth it, Adeline.'

12

It wasn't.

'Addie?' I called, playing snatches from her song from time to time in hopes that one or the other sound would penetrate the forest gloaming.

No answer came, and she did not appear. I trudged through tangled thickets of conifer trees, their trunks wound about with ivy so dark green in hue it was almost black. Pools of water hid beneath the carpeting brambles, the one wetting my feet and the other scratching my ankles and legs, and progress was slow. How had Addie managed to disappear so thoroughly with such terrain to hamper her?

Magickal faerie creature. Right.

At last I heard a faint whinny, and another, and I adjusted my steps accordingly.

But it was not Addie that had called. It was another unicorn.

Another two minutes' trudging brought me to the edge of a shadowy glade. There the trees grew more sparsely, and grass rather than bramble and vine covered the ground. In the centre was a serene pool, its glassy surface darkened.

Around the edges of that pool stood a whole herd of unicorns. I counted at least twelve, including Adeline.

She was making enthusiastic friends with a great, golden-palomino stallion.

Very enthusiastic friends.

'Oh,' I said.

I turned away my eyes, and sidled up to the pool, for a glimmer of something had caught my eye.

There, submerged at the bottom of the clear waters, was the most exquisite lyre. Smaller than most, its arched, curving frame looked made from moonlight itself: the moonsilver was aptly named. It appeared unstrung, but what had Mother said about it? Strung with enchanted waters from the king's own pools.

Was this one of those pools?

Either way, what was it doing here, instead of up on the hilltop with the rest of the lost king's personal effects?

My feet being soaked anyway, I shrugged and began to wade into the water.

'*Stop.*' My mother's voice split the clearing like a whiplash, and I stopped on reflex.

'What—'

'Remember what happened when you tried to take the pipes off the bier?' Mother and Jay had made it as far as the glade, but they remained on the edge of it, well away from the unicorn herd and the pool. Both looked disquieted.

'Yes, but this has nothing of the same appearance. Look at it. All lop-sided as though someone just chucked it in there.'

'They probably did. And what would encourage a person to hurl a Great Treasure to the bottom of a pool, do you suppose?'

'Nothing good. Even so—'

'Never mind *even so*. Leave it alone.'

I felt a flash of irritation. 'Mother. You've dragged us all the way out here in order to find this damned lyre and the man who once played it. No? Well, we've found one of them. There it is, right there! And now you want me to just walk away?'

'Yes. We've found it; excellent. And that's enough.'

'We can't just leave it here. The Yllanfalen will want it back.'

'You think they don't know exactly where it is?'

I frowned. 'They said it was missing.'

'Yep. All of them, over and over, using almost the same words. We suspected there was something shady about it, no? Come on, Ves. Fight it off.'

'Fight what off?'

'The lyre,' said Jay. 'Has a hold of you somehow. If you could see your own face—'

'What's wrong with my face?'

'Nothing,' said Jay peaceably. 'But there's something a little bit wrong with your eyes.'

'Namely?'

'They're the wrong colour.'

'And they're what colour now?'

Jay pointed towards the moon-pale lyre glimmering with its silvery glow. 'That colour.'

So I had moonsilver eyes.

Right.

Only then did I realise that the pipes around my neck were glowing faintly with a similar light.

Mother pointed imperiously at Adeline. 'Unicorn,' she said sternly. 'You've led your friend into danger. Now get her out of it.'

The unicorns, indeed, seemed untouched by whatever weird fae magick was going on in that glade. Possibly they were a part of it; certainly they were attracted to it.

Adeline stamped one hoof, and snorted.

'If my daughter comes a-cropper in this glade,' said Mother darkly, 'I shall cut off your tail.'

Adeline's ears twitched.

'And you'd deserve it.'

Slowly, with the demeanour of a scolded child, Adeline wended her way around the pool's edge until she reached me.

Then, with deliberate and tender care, she bit my ear.

'*Ouch*,' I shrieked, as much with surprise as with pain.

But something shattered, and unwound. I felt as though I'd been doused in ice-cold water, suddenly alert. I became abruptly aware of the frigid temperature of the pool I was standing in up to my calves, and backed out of the water so fast I almost fell over.

Hands grabbed me and pulled me farther free: Jay had hold of me.

'All right,' he said calmly, once he had pulled me all the way back to the glade's edge. He gave me a considering once-over. 'You look nearly normal again.'

'Nearly?'

He indicated the pipes in my left hand, which were still softly aglow.

'I'm getting confused,' I said. 'Are these the king's pipes, or was that the set up on the hill?'

'This isn't a story,' said Jay, lips curving with faint amusement. 'Why can't the king have more than one set of special magick pipes? Maybe he made them both.'

'Quite likely,' said Mother. 'Cordelia. What I was going to tell you before your mad dash to inevitable doom: those winds that blew up, those were Winds of the Ways. There are strong traces of Waymagick all over the hill and the forest both. Faded, to be sure — at least decades old. But there's no mistaking it.'

'So there must be a henge somewhere here?' I said.

She nodded. 'It's my guess that whoever threw the lyre into the pool left by the Winds. But,' she added, holding up a hand to forestall my response, 'I don't think that person was a Waymaster.'

'What? How can you tell?'

'Because the place is crawling with faerie magick, too.'

'Hardly surprising. It's a faerie glade, Mother.'

'Yes, but even the fae don't throw magick around willy-nilly without a purpose.'

'The Winds aren't what I'm used to,' said Jay. 'They're more... playful, unstable, erratic. Like they've been summoned by an unfocused mind, or—'

'By lots of minds,' I supplied.

He nodded. 'And whoever it is has been mucking about with them, like they're a toy.'

'Sounds very fae.'

'Specifically,' said Mother, 'sounds very sprite.'

Of course. The music-seller had said the sprites tend gardens; from Ayllin we knew that they kept the doors, among other things — and they did not often show themselves. Were the glade and the forest awash with them?

'Did they throw the lyre in the water?' I speculated.

'Maybe,' said Mother. 'But maybe not. It's hard to sense under all the fae magick, but someone human's worked enchantments here in the past.'

'Your lyre-player?'

She shrugged. 'No way to know.'

'Can you catch these Winds?' I said to Jay.

'Yes. If we find the henge.'

'Will you?'

'If someone gave me good reason to.' He folded his arms and gave me his sceptical look.

'I want to find out where they go.'

'And then do what?'

I shrugged.

'Don't you ever get tired of playing Trial and Error?'

'Nope.' I smiled.

'This is the henge,' said Mother.

Jay looked sharply at her. 'Are you sure? I don't see it.'

I realised that when Jay said "see" he meant with his Waymaster senses. It wouldn't be the first time we had used a buried henge with no visible stones or earthworks.

'Might be fairer to say it used to be a henge,' said Mother. 'But the residue's still here.'

Jay nodded. 'We can try it.' He took a hold of me, and beckoned to Mother.

'Just a second,' said she, and stepped into the glade.

The unicorns had drifted away, and stood in a cluster on the far side of the pool, idly munching grass. At first I thought Mother was heading for them, perhaps Adeline specifically.

But no. Her path led her unerringly to the pool of water I had so lately been hauled out of. And she didn't hesitate. She waded right in, up to her ankles, her calves, her knees.

'Mother!' I called, and ran for her. 'What are you *doing*?'

She made it to the centre before I could reach the edge of the water. Quick as a flash, she plunged her healthy hand into the pool and snatched up the lyre.

I was wading in after her by then. 'Mum, you bloody madwoman, what did you *just* say to me?' I grabbed her and began hauling her backwards, hoping she would drop the lyre.

She didn't. 'I told *you* to leave it alone,' she said, in a voice of grim satisfaction. 'Didn't say anything about me.'

'Isn't that just the way with parents,' I growled as we stumbled out of the water. 'A thousand rules for me, none whatsoever for you. *What have you done?*'

I looked full into her face, expecting to see that moon-silver shine in her eyes that Jay had described in mine. But it was not there. Her own, hazel eyes stared back at me, just the same as they always were. Not a hint of faerie glamour could I detect.

As far as I could tell, my mother had acted voluntarily.

'Tell you later.' She stuffed the lyre under one arm, where its strings of rippling water promptly soaked through her sleeve.

Oh well. She and I both were thoroughly drenched by then anyway.

'Shall we go?' She was looking at Jay, who had adopted his Bleak Stare.

'Why did you do that?' he said.

'My daughter is right, we cannot just leave the lyre there.'

'So why did you stop her from taking it?'

'Because when it comes to faerie treasures, there's always a consequence. A woman may weather the effects of one faerie instrument well enough. Not two.'

I rolled my eyes. 'So you were protecting me. How nice.'

'Is it so hard to believe?'

'Yes.'

She scowled. 'So, are we going?'

Jay's eyes narrowed, but what more could he say? The damage, whatever it might prove to be, had been done.

'Just keep the thing away from Ves,' he said. 'The second I see her eyes turn all moonish again, we're throwing it away.'

Mum clutched at it like he'd have to remove her other hand first.

Jay returned her a stare that said, *try me.*

13

I MIGHT BE BECOMING an old hand at travelling by the Ways, but this was something else.

We were whirled up, up and away into the aether; so far, so ordinary. After that, we were leaves on the wind, and not in a cute way. Ever watched a coppery autumn leaf tossing and turning in the currents, sailing with airy serenity from gust to gust? It looks like the epitome of freedom.

It feels like crap.

As if the Winds themselves weren't "playful" enough (as Jay had euphemistically put it), invisible hands snatched at my clothes, my limbs, my hair, and sent me tumbling in dizzying spirals. After half a miserable minute of this, I was longing for solid ground beneath my feet and praying, otherwise, to die.

When at last the whirl of winds ceased, and I felt approximately stationary again, the first words to pass my lips were: 'A *pox* on all sprites. One of the really bad ones, too.'

'Smallpox,' said my mother.

'Too... small.'

'The Black Death,' said Jay.

'Might do.'

'Actually,' came a new and unfamiliar voice, 'they're sylphs.'

I opened my eyes.

Considering the starting point and our mode of transport, I'd expected to end up somewhere else improbably beautiful, even if it ended up being another clone of Hansel and Gretel's forest.

Instead, we'd landed in somebody's living room. I felt carpet under my hands — reasonably plush, not cheap — and the ceiling I was staring at was white plaster, with fussy ornaments in the corners. A huge bookcase monopolised the far wall, and tucked into the corner was a standard lamp with a kingfisher-blue shade, and a deep, luxurious armchair.

In the armchair sat a man of, maybe, sixty. His hair was grey, his face rather tanned, his eyes extraordinary: a kind of silvery-blue colour. He looked unassuming, in his wine-coloured jumper and dark trousers, with a large book open on his lap. His stare, though, was penetrating.

'I appear to be horizontal,' I said.

'It's rare to encounter the sylphs and come out standing,' said the man.

I looked around, wincing around a pain in my neck. Jay had already made it to his feet, and stood with his back to the window, looking rather... trapped.

Mother had dragged herself into a corner, like a wounded animal, and sat scowling at the person we'd inadvertently gate-crashed upon.

'Have I changed that much?' she growled.

The man closed his book and turned a thoughtful stare upon Mother. 'When a trio of hitch-hikers wash up without warning in my living room, it's rather too much to expect to know them as well.'

'Just one,' said Mother. 'Just me.'

I sat up, and peered at the man with unabashed scepticism. *This* was the gorgeous lyre-player? He looked ready to become somebody's kindly grandfather about now, or he would if it wasn't for that steely stare.

'Mum,' I said. 'This can't be him.'

'It is,' she said.

'It can't be.'

'I know, but it is.'

'Mother. He's either under the best fae glamour I've ever heard of, or he's human.'

'You've come from the rath?' said the man, ignoring this exchange.

'The what?' said Mother.

'The fort. Is my effigy still there?'

I stared. '*Your* effigy?' I blurted.

'I'll take that as a yes.' He smiled, faint and wintry.

I clutched, involuntarily, at my pipes, which proved to be a poor move. His eyes zoned in on them immediately, and if I thought he'd looked intimidating before... 'You took my pipes?' he said.

'These aren't your pipes,' I said hastily. 'At least, they might be, but they're not the ones from the rath. And anyway those aren't your pipes either, they can't be, because they're the king's pipes and you aren't the king.'

He endured my babbling with enviable serenity and only said: 'Am I not?'

'You're human.'

'What's that got to do with anything?'

I blinked. 'Who ever heard of a human faerie king?'

'Every man, woman and child in Yllanfalen, more's the pity.' The man opened his book again, and went back to reading.

A glance at my mother's face suggested she was as impressed with this conduct as I was.

So I threw my pipes at him.

Okay, not *at* him, quite. They landed harmlessly in his lap.

'All right,' said his rudeness, the purported faerie king. 'Why are you here?' He picked up the pipes and subjected them to close scrutiny. I saw his eyes widen a fraction, though he quickly hid his reaction.

'We came looking for you,' said Mother.

'I gathered that. Why?'

'I told you. I know you.'

He played a few notes on my pipes, just enough to instantly lay my pride in the dust. With ten years of practice, I thought I had got pretty good at the art.

If I was pretty good, he was a maestro. Under his hands, my little pipes produced a sound of such aching beauty, I felt tears spring to my eyes.

I *hate* emotionally manipulative music.

As he played, he stared unblinking at my mother's face, and slowly shook his head.

'Does this help?' said my mother. She withdrew the lyre from under her arm, held it up, and let its full radiance shine.

And, oh, shine it did. It shone like the moon.

The king-who-might-not-be dropped the pipes, and silence reigned.

Then, he put his face in his hands. The muffled words, 'Oh gods, no,' emerged.

'Not the response I was hoping for,' muttered Mother.

'Thirty years,' said he, without removing his hands. 'Thirty years, and no one's been foolish enough to remove that thing.'

The thing in question was busy being so indescribably beautiful, I was wounded on its behalf at so unflattering an epithet. I sat and watched it shine, entranced. The strings really were water. They rippled, and they were faintly pearly, like moonlight on the river...

'*Yes,*' snapped Jay, and interposed himself between me and the lyre. He snapped his fingers in front of my face. 'Your eyes are changing again. Focus.'

'Fine, I'll put it away,' said Mother.

'Best do, or I'll feed it to the nearest sewer-grate.'

'At last, someone with sense,' said the maybe-king. He narrowed his eyes at Mother. 'You were there, weren't you. That night at the halls.'

Mother rolled her eyes. 'Yes, I was *present*.'

'Delia.'

She went quiet, and finally said, 'You do remember.'

'Yes.' He didn't entirely look pleased about it.

'But you weren't human, that night,' said Mother.

'Glamoured. My own face, only better. More beautiful... you know how it works,' he finished with a scowl.

'Mhm.' Mother apparently went into an appreciative reverie.

'Are you the king of the Yllanfalen or are you not?' said Jay, in tones of exasperation.

'No,' said the man.

'Then what have you been talking about?'

He threw aside his book. 'I *was*, until I managed to get rid of that damned lyre.'

'What's the lyre got to do with it?' I said.

'Everything.'

I looked from him to Mother, deeply confused. Nobody had even touched on the topic of his possible fatherhood, yet, and I wasn't sure I wanted to. I saw nothing in his face that reminded me of my own, but what did that signify?

I detected a shade of uncertainty in my mother's eyes.

'Perhaps you'd be good enough to explain,' said Jay, with a politeness that seemed a trifle forced.

'I will do that,' said the erstwhile faerie king, 'once I understand what *you* are doing in my living room.'

No one spoke. Jay and I were waiting for Mother to explain, but she sat cradling that mischievous lyre in silence, her face impassive.

I sighed. 'We came looking for... the lyre. Or you. Or both.' I waved a hand at my silent parent. 'All her idea. Jay and I are still catching up.'

'Great girl, my daughter,' said Mother, placing a slight emphasis on the last word.

'I'm not a girl, mother. Hit womanhood quite a while ago.'

'This is your girl, hm?' said the not-king.

I gave up the point. 'Mum, if you're waiting for him to figure it out on his own, we could be here a while. Could we maybe save some time?'

Mother rolled her eyes, and strummed her fingers lightly over the lyre's watery strings. 'Cordelia was born about eight and a half months after that night,' she said.

Well, that got Dad's attention. He reeled back as though she'd thrown something at him, and stared at me in dawning horror.

'Hallo, Father,' I said, casually tossing back my hair.

My show of nonchalance did not fool Jay, at least. He drew nearer to me, as though closing ranks against the parental complications. I appreciated that.

'That's impossible,' my maybe-father gasped.

'Biologically speaking, it's highly probable,' said Mother.

'But not definite?' I disliked how quick the wretched man was to leap on that point.

Mother studiously avoided my eye. 'The other alternative is rather less likely.'

So much for Richard Rosser. No wonder he'd never contacted me.

'So you brought her here to meet me.' There still wasn't a trace of welcome or joy discernible in his face, and I developed a sudden, fervent desire to tear my mother's other hand off with my teeth.

One's ego can only take so much in the way of a beating.

'Yes...' said Mother, and you can bet all three of us caught the hesitation in the word.

Finding three pairs of eyes fixed upon her, Mother gave up all in a rush. She lifted the lyre, waved it at me — at *me* — and said: 'It's about Cordelia meeting her father, but it's also about this. If she is your daughter, then... then this, and everything it signifies, is her birth right.'

I gritted my teeth. 'And what does the lyre signify, Mother?'

'Ohgod.' That was Jay. He looked like he wanted to copy my father's fine example, and put his face in his hands. 'You said the lyre had everything to do with the monarchy. It's not that the king gets the instruments as some kind of perk, is it? Whoever owns the instruments *is the king.*'

'Or the queen, in this case,' said Mother, with a smug quirk of her lips.

I backed up so fast, and so far, that my back hit the wall with a *thud.* 'Oh, no. No way, absolutely definitely *not,* you have got to be joking...' I shook my head vigorously. 'No. You said anyone can play the lyre on festival days! Anybody!'

'Anyone can play it,' said Mother inflexibly. 'I also said, no one else could play it like *that*.'

I hadn't heard my father play the lyre, but if he played it the way he'd played my pipes, then fair enough.

'But I can't play the pipes half so well,' I objected. 'If musical talent is an indicator of royalty then I'm out.'

'Because they haven't chosen yet,' said Mother placidly. 'It's not about musical talent at all. It's about— oh, you explain.' She cast an irritable glance at my father.

He sat back, wide-eyed with amazement. Or amusement, damn him. 'These instruments were made by King Evelaern himself, long ages ago,' he said. 'Your mother is right: it is an ancient ritual and an ancient spell. When one monarch is ready to pass on the crown, the instruments choose another. No one knows how.' His lips twisted. 'It hasn't always been that simple.'

'Why then didn't you just let me pick up the lyre, if this has been the plan all along?' I said to Mother.

'I wanted to make sure your father was ready to hand on the crown, first.'

'But— but—' I was floundering. 'But what do bloodlines have to do with any of this?'

'Nothing,' said Father flatly.

'It's passed down family lines before,' said Mother stubbornly.

Father raised a brow at her. 'Has it?'

'I've researched the matter.'

He grimaced. 'Done your homework. Very good.'

'*Why*, Mother?' I said. 'Why by all the giddy gods would you want to install me as queen of some damned faerie kingdom?'

She looked at me like I was crazy. 'Cordelia. You spent fully half your childhood playing at being the Faerie Queene.'

'Just games! I was a child!'

'But were they? Maybe it was your heritage speaking.'

'Have you been planning this ever since?'

'No. Only for the last half a dozen years.'

Having run out of words, I could only stare at her, flabbergasted.

Father held up a hand. 'I feel I ought to enlighten you on one or two points.'

Jay said, 'You mentioned it isn't always simple.'

Father nodded. 'Never less so than when I was chosen. I'd better tell you the story.'

14

'THE YLLANFALEN ARE A fine people, all told,' my Father began. 'Noble, enlightened, highly talented. But where there is power, there will always be those with a desire to seize it at any cost. So it was thirty years ago, when the old king passed and the time came for another to step into the role.

'I'd travelled into the kingdom of Yllanfalen because I was a student of music at the time, and of magick. I wanted to develop the combined arts, and where better to do that? They are rightly legendary for their prowess at magickal melody and song. I knew nothing about the succession, and cared less. I just wanted to play.

'And play I did, when my turn came around. What I did not know was that the lyre had been, by some means, corrupted, before it fell into my hands. Its ancient song no longer worked as intended. Instead of selecting a suitable monarch by its own judgement, it would simply bestow the crown on the next person to play it. It was meant to fall into other hands than mine; by some accident, I received it instead.

'But it did not choose me, nor did I choose to accept the role. I didn't want it. The night dissolved into chaos after that, for I was unpopular with *everyone.* She who had intended to take up the lyre and the monarchy both was furious with me, as you may imagine. The rest of the Yllanfalen were furious with us, too: me for being human, and the lyre for daring to install one over them as ruler.

'They declared the lyre broken, and me an exile. Well, I was happy to go! I tried to leave the lyre with the effigy of old King Evelaern on the hill, but I couldn't, somehow. So I threw it into the water. I found that the sprites were minded to obey me; exile I might be, but I was still the king by their law. So they took me home, and... I have never been back there since.'

I digested all this in silence for a moment. 'So when they said the king had passed, they meant they'd thrown him out.'

'They were probably speaking of the old king. Many among the Yllanfalen still consider the lyre's last choice invalid, and fairly enough. I wasn't really chosen.'

Jay said, 'And they're so happy with the idea of a human for a king, they'd rather have none at all.'

Father smiled faintly. 'If you consider how superior they look to our eyes, only imagine how inferior we appear to theirs.'

Mother was silent among the wreckage of all her wild plans. When I saw the look of utter dismay in her eyes, I lost some of my desire to eviscerate her. Six years' work crushed inside of three minutes.

Father wasn't so kind. 'So you see, Delia, your daugh-ter—'

'*Our* daughter,' she interrupted, almost snarling the words.

'—has no right to the monarchy at all, and they would never accept her even if she did. Such dreams ought to be put away.'

Mother shrugged, and offered me the lyre. 'She can still have the lyre to go with those pipes. The Yllanfalen don't seem to want it anyway.'

I put my hands behind my back. 'No thanks. That thing scares the living daylights out of me.'

Jay, though, interceded — and not quite on my behalf. 'Ves, the fact that you're the only one who seems so drawn to it... that might be significant.'

'What.'

'The way your eyes reflect its light. Why? There's some kind of connection between you and it that neither your mother nor I are subject to.'

'Neither is your father,' Mother put in.

'Doesn't mean it's a good connection,' I argued. 'And it's probably just responding to the palpable greed in my little heart whenever anything shiny is put before me.'

'That could be it,' Jay allowed, with a faint smile.

'How did you get those pipes?' said my father, with a sudden, sharp look.

'Your unicorn,' said Mother.

But he shook his head. 'I wasn't king long enough to form any bonds with the unicorns. If she's got one of those trailing around after her, it'd be a former king in question. If any.'

'Maybe Addie just likes me,' I said. All in all, I much preferred that idea.

Mother held out the lyre to me, and said, with a deep weariness, 'Please. Just take it. Apart from anything, I promised Milady.'

'You promised Milady what?'

'I promised the Society the use of the lyre, if we got hold of it. Why not? If you claimed it, you'd surely share.'

The possibility that Milady and my mother had conspired together to shove me onto a faerie throne did not much improve my mood. I opened my mouth to express some of this.

My expression of simmering rage apparently tipped my mother off, for she held up her stump. 'No, I didn't let her in on the queen-of-all-faeries plan.'

Queen of All Faeries. I distantly remembered awarding myself that title, around about age five, during many of my solitary games. I was hardly the only child to do so, surely. What was *wrong* with my reprehensible mother?

'I'm sorry, Delia,' said Jay firmly, 'but I think we'll have to disappoint Milady. That lyre has to go back to the Ylanfalen.'

She blinked up at him in shock. 'But they don't want it. You heard the man.'

'It's Thomas,' said my father. 'In case anyone was interested.'

'I am,' I said. 'Thomas what?'

'Thomas Goldwell.'

I offered my hand, which he took, and we shook hands with exquisite politeness. 'How nice to meet you, Mr. Goldwell.'

'And you, Miss... Goldwell.'

Was that my name, then? Cordelia Goldwell?

Nah. I'd been Vesper all my life.

But hey, a proposed name-change was a vast improvement over the horror with which he'd earlier looked upon me.

'Call me Ves,' I said.

'Tom, then.'

That settled, I was at leisure to attend to the argument unfolding between Jay and my mother. He was in favour of the lyre's return, she staunchly against. The battle looked set to rage on for some time, and the combatants were evenly matched: my mother's gritty, rock-solid stubbornness against Jay's calm logic and inflexible morality.

I'd privately put my money on Jay.

'But they *don't want it*,' shouted Mother, like it was at least the sixth time she'd said it.

'That is beside the point,' said Jay, raising his own voice more than is usual for him. 'It is rightfully theirs. And if they don't want it, it's only because it's been broken. They *do* want what it was before.'

'We can't just unbreak it,' said Mother scornfully. 'It's broken for good. So if they don't want the broken one, why can't we have it?'

'It needs to be mended!'

'Do you have any idea how to do that? Because if the Yllanfalen did, don't you think they'd have done it by now?'

I had to admit, that point of my mother's was a hard one to answer.

But Jay had it all under control. 'I'd say there's one person who could mend it, perhaps with a little help. The problem is, the Yllanfalen didn't want to have anything to do with him. *We* have no such feelings.'

Everyone looked at Tom, who held up his hands. 'I will have nothing to do with this.'

'Why not?' I said.

Silence fell, and my father looked consternated. 'Well — you heard. They threw me out. I'm forbidden from ever setting foot in Yllanfalen again.'

'Why? For being human?' I said.

'That, and I think they believe *I* was the one who corrupted the lyre.'

'You weren't, were you?' said Jay, with a narrow look.

'No. I swear it. Only a madman could imagine the Yllanfalen would accept a human for a ruler.'

'And only a madwoman would want to be queen of a faerie kingdom, for real,' I snapped.

'You're serious,' said Mother.

'Utterly.'

She grumbled something inaudible. 'Then you can explain to Milady about the lyre.'

'Gladly.'

One parent down, one to go. 'Dad?' I said.

He visibly flinched.

'We are going to need you.'

'You cannot make this into my problem if I do not choose to permit it,' he said, snapping straight back into his icy-cold routine.

'It is already your problem,' I said. 'It's been your problem for thirty years.'

'Don't you want to be able to forget about the lyre?' said Jay. 'Forever? Help us, and it won't be your problem ever again.'

Father tossed aside his book. 'There are days when I wish I just hadn't woken up at all.'

'Could turn out to be the best day ever,' I said with a bright smile. 'You've already found a daughter.'

Father did not look as though this had been as transformative an experience for him as I might like. He stood up, and did a spectacular double-take in my mother's general direction. 'What,' he said in a terrible voice, 'happened to your hand?'

Mother gave her wolf-grin. 'Why don't I tell you about it on the way.'

So, BACK WE WENT. To Cumbria; to Sheep Island; to the extinct gnome village, and to the caverns beneath (now with fewer lindworms!).

Mum made Dad carry the lyre.

He wasn't happy about it.

The lyre, though, clearly was. It sang all by itself, without cease, adjusting its airy melodies to the circumstances as it saw fit.

And so it was, that our reluctantly heroic quartet set off in search of adventure with our own theme music to accompany us.

I keep thinking there'll come a day when life will get a little simpler — or at least less absurd? Dream on.

'What happened with you and your mother?' said Jay at one point, somewhere en route.

'Nothing?' I said. 'Which is sort of the problem.'

'But she talks as though you two were close, when you were a child.'

'If we were, I don't remember anything about it. She sent me to boarding school at the age of six.'

'That's... young.'

'Rather.'

'Why would she do that?'

I could only shrug. 'Jay, you're the product of a solid marriage where both parties wanted to become parents. Or so I assume. I'm the product of a drunken one-night stand between two deeply irresponsible people. Why my mother didn't just abort me I will never understand.'

'Maybe she decided she liked the idea of parenthood after all.'

'Then changed her mind after a few years? All too possible.'

'Aren't you glad she went through with it, even so? I know I am.'

He'd earned a smile with that one, so I bestowed my best one. 'Thanks. Yes, I suppose I am.'

'Though I wish you'd had a better childhood.'

'Apparently it's not entirely vital after all. I turned out fine.'

Jay was silent after that. Whether that was because he'd said everything he wanted to say on the subject, or whether he privately disagreed with my assessment of my character in adulthood, I decided not to ask.

I *did* turn out fine... right?

These were the thoughts that occupied my mind as we wandered back into the King's Halls, our party augmented by one king. I should've been paying more attention, though, for we were little more than halfway across the cellars when mother abruptly stopped and said: 'Lindworm.'

'What?' I gulped. 'I can't—'

'It's fine.' My father took up the moonsilver lyre, played exactly three perfect notes, and while the crashing sounds of a lindworm on the approach rent the air, he stood with perfect composure and waited.

It came on in a rush, jaws agape, and looked ready to devour my father in one gulp.

Dad played those three notes again, and said in a ringing voice: 'No.'

The lindworm stopped dead, closed its jaws with a snap, and then — I kid you not — it put its great head in the dirt and literally grovelled before my irascible parent.

'Go,' said Father. 'Leave these halls to me.'

And the lindworm went.

'Was there something?' said Father, in response to our three-way stare.

'Nothing,' I squeaked.

'It's good to be the king,' said Mother, with a sideways glance at me.

And damn her, she wasn't wrong.

15

'Now that we're here,' I said, as we trudged upstairs towards the grander halls, 'how does one go about mending the lyre?'

'I don't know, precisely,' said my father. 'But it is to do with its song. Something has been altered in its melody.

'Which means what?'

'Means it needs to remember how it used to sing.'

'Vague.'

'It is the best I've got.'

'Then we'll take it. Are these old songs recorded somewhere, by chance?'

'That is my hope. There used to be a library, of sorts.'

'I love libraries.'

He smiled sideways at me. 'We have that in common. But the library I speak of is not quite what you're thinking. This is the Library of Music, and while it has some books of written melodies, the majority of its collections are composed of other records.'

'Such as?'

'You'll see.'

On our previous visits, the King's Halls had been so absolutely empty that we'd grown careless, traipsing about the place like we owned it.

When we arrived at the Library of Music, that changed. We'd heard the distant strains of faerie melodies as we'd walked, growing nearer and louder with every step; 'That is not unusual,' Father had said. 'There is always music in the Library, with or without anyone to play it.' But as we stepped over the threshold, we found that Tom was right — and also wrong.

I saw at once what he had meant about "other records". Melodies hung all about the doorway as we entered the vaulted chamber, strung together like chains of bubbles — or beads. I reached out to one, touched it; I couldn't resist, any more than I could resist caressing a particularly beautiful book. The moment my fingers brushed its iridescent blue shell, it sparked with a pale light, and a lilting song filled my mind, sung by a hundred voices. It had an air of antiquity about it, and I judged it early modern in era.

There was no restraining myself after that, of course, for they were everywhere: wafting in puffs of light and mist from wall to wall, clustering in multitudes under the ceiling, and filling up the corners. Some attempt had been made to organise them, for the large, square room was fitted with a great number of clear glass cabinets; behind those locked doors waited many a melody, bobbing to their own tunes. But the quantity had far outpaced the librarians' efforts to store them, and the result was a charming chaos. I went through it like a pig in a cake shop, greedily absorbing melody after melody until my ears rang and I could scarce hear myself think.

Jay was just as enchanted as I. 'Indira has to see this place,' he enthused, his dark eyes alight.

'Oh? Is she musical, too?'

'We all are.'

'All the Patels? What a talented family you do have.'

'Music is a skill to be mastered, like any other.'

'No doubt, but you do seem to have mastered an unusual quantity of skills between you, and at a young age to boot.'

'I don't sleep much.'

Neither did Indira, apparently. Was that by choice or happenstance? If by choice: why were they *so* driven?

And just how many siblings did Jay have, anyway?

Before I could ask any of these questions, though — once again displaying my splendid talent for getting distracted from the main point — a dry voice interrupted us. 'Were you looking for anything in particular?'

So absorbed had we been, we had failed to notice that a large chair in one corner was occupied. It hadn't even occurred to us that we might find someone else in the library. My parents were having a low-voiced argument in another part of the room, but they, too, stopped mid-sentence and observed the librarian in surprise.

If librarian she was. She had an appearance to draw the eye, being shorter even than me, and withered, but in the way that ancient trees are withered. Her skin was dark, dark brown, almost black, and her eyes the same; her hair, though, was an airy white, and drifted about her head like wisps of summer cloud. She was wearing a pair of old grey jeans, with a long cardigan over the top that looked hand-knitted. Hardly could she have been more different from the elegant Yllanfalen, or more incongruous a presence in that room of ethereal melody and magick.

I looked for signs of hostility in her face, or her tone, but there was none. Her eyes smiled at us, and I wondered what she had found so amusing in our behaviour.

'We've come about the lyre,' I said, when neither of my parents seemed disposed to explain themselves.

'The lyre?' said she.

'The moonsilver lyre. Lyre of kings and queens.'

'Has it come back, then?' she said, with interest but without surprise. 'It's about time.'

'Is it? I thought it was no longer welcome here. Was it not thrown away?'

'Aye! And a greater piece of foolishness I cannot think of.'

'Well,' said my father, and held out the lyre. 'Here it is. If you know how to mend it, I beg you'd assist us, for we can find nothing in this mess.'

The amusement gleamed more brightly in her eyes, and white teeth flashed in a grin. 'Rather a shambles, isn't it?' she agreed. 'But it's a pretty mess, for all that. Was it the king's old songs you wanted?'

'Any that it used to sing, before it was changed. I thought that might help.'

'Changed?' The withered woman tilted her head. 'Has it been?'

'Naturally,' said father. 'For it would never otherwise have chosen me.'

'Would it not?'

'Of course not.'

'Ah. You are unqualified, in some obscure way, for the role.'

'In every way, I would say.'

'But it seems the lyre would not.'

'It was not... thinking clearly, if we may suppose that it thinks.'

Her head tilted again. 'Was it not?'

Father grew impatient. 'You cannot tell me the Old King's Moonsilver Lyre deliberately chose a human to fill his shoes.'

'I will not, then, if the idea offends you.' She was laughing again.

'It offended the Yllanfalen.'

'It offended some of them. If the lyre did not mind it, then why should you?'

Father set the lyre onto a table, and gave a great, weary sigh. 'I don't want to be king of this place.'

'Ahhh. Then we get to the real trouble.'

'Indeed.'

'Few are given the right to choose their own course in life. Our paths are as much chosen for us, as by us.'

'I'm choosing not to take this one,' said Father firmly.

The withered woman nodded. 'And you'd like the lyre to choose someone else.'

'Yes. I've been hiding from the damned thing for thirty years, and my daughter imagines it might be possible to stop.'

Those bright black eyes flicked to me, and stayed there.

I tried to look wise and innocent in equal measure, and probably failed equally too. 'That and I thought the Yllanfalen might like to have a king again.'

'They have done very well without one.'

'Have they, though? Look at this place. Abandoned, ignored. All their ancient culture is seeping away, and they're letting it go.'

'If that is their choice, why does it matter to you?'

'I protect culture, and tradition, and history. It is my job, my purpose... I don't understand why a people would let theirs slip away like this. I cannot believe that they really wish it.'

'Perhaps they don't, at that.' The woman leapt out of her chair, so suddenly as to startle me, and I took an involuntary step back. She seemed overflowing with energy, despite her apparently advanced age, and I felt in that moment that she could achieve anything. 'Let us try to mend a culture, then, shall we? And see what comes of it.'

'Who exactly are you?' snapped my mother. 'Do you have aid to give, or just weighty words?'

'She's a sprite,' said Father.

The sprite cackled in a fashion I found decidedly unspriteish. 'I am Cadence,' she said. 'I and my sisters can help you find the Old King's songs.'

'Sisters?' said Father faintly.

'I am Descant,' said a second voice.

'And I am Euphony,' said a third.

I whirled to find two more sprites appeared out of nowhere: both shorter still than Cadence, one with skin as purple as a ripe beet, and the other as pale as me. I could not guess which was which. They were both ancient; an unforgiving fairy tale would have termed them haggish. But they were as merry and quick as their sister, and as sharp, I judged.

To my surprise, these two bowed before my father and said: 'Majesty.'

'I'm not your king,' he growled.

Their eyes strayed to the lyre sitting meekly atop the nearby table. 'But the lyre says—'

'And should a pile of enchanted metal make all your important decisions for you?' he said.

'It is the way of things,' said the pale one (Descant?)

'Hush, Euphony,' said Cadence. 'It is unwise to argue with kings.'

'But you did! A moment ago! I heard you.'

'Aye! And it is the king's will that I shut my mouth and bend my wits to the task at hand.' Her laughter was back, squarely directed at my father.

'The sooner then you may be rid of me,' said Father calmly.

'We don't want to be rid of you,' said Descant. 'It's dull here all alone. We want the music back.'

'You have every imaginable strain and song in here.' Father gestured vaguely at the plethora of magickal musics drifting every which way. 'Is this not enough for you?'

'They are echoes,' Descant replied. 'Like memories. Imagine if you had only memory left, nothing real—'

'I would love for you to have your kingdom back the way it was,' Father interrupted. 'But not with me at the head of it. I will do everything I can to help you replace me. Fair?'

Descant looked ready to argue, but a warning look from Cadence silenced her, and she bowed her head. 'Only it is perfectly king-shaped already,' she muttered rebelliously, almost too quietly to be heard.

'It is!' said Euphony. 'Tall enough, to be sure! And the lyre loves it.'

'It does not love the lyre.'

'It is a fool.'

'Shall we want a fool for a king?'

'Why should a fool not be a king? It has come about before.'

'But is it a *good* king? Shall we want one that is not a fool?'

'A wise fool? A merry fool?'

'A cross fool! Look at the face. It despises us.'

Father took a breath. 'Can we just get on with it? Please? I've a book to finish.'

Cadence waved her sisters to silence. 'The old king's old songs. Old, old, old. Find them all.'

'Is it better to be old?' whispered Descant. 'If so, we're in a fine space, sisters.'

'Always better,' said Euphony wisely. 'The King says so.'

'I didn't say that—' protested Father. 'Oh, for goodness' sake.'

Mother, to my surprise, laughed. 'I like you,' she said to the sprites.'

'It is missing a hand,' said Euphony to Cadence, and waved about both of her own. 'How does it play?'

'It doesn't,' said mother. 'But then it never did, particularly. It's my daughter that's the musical one. And she's got the king's pipes, look.'

All three sprites surveyed me, with expressions deeply thoughtful, and — speculative.

'Shall we have this one for the king, then?' said Descant.

'It looks merry enough,' said Euphony.

Cadence smiled broadly at me.

'Oh, for goodness' sake,' I said, for my father's words seemed to sum up the situation nicely. 'Can we all please get off that idea?'

16

Some half an hour later, a period of intense search on the part of the three sprites, and the four of us as well, it was Descant who suddenly screamed, 'I FOUND IT!'

Her sisters rushed to her side, as did Jay and I, though there was nothing to see. She had hold of a fine, large bubble in her small fist, its shell pearly-white, and she waved it around in triumph. 'It's the oldest of all the old ones! Here, Cadence, see if it isn't the oldest.' And she delivered the melody into her sister's hands with a flourish.

Cadence considered it closely. 'It is well-found, Descant. We will see if the lyre remembers.'

'How old is the lyre?' asked Jay.

I looked at it, but being unfamiliar with Yllanfalen aesthetic history I was unable to determine anything to the purpose at all. Except that it was pretty. So very, very pretty... its curves shone moon-bright, and its strings flowed like sunglow on the sea—

'Ves,' said Jay, and gently turned me around until my back was to the lyre.

'Thanks,' I sighed. '*Why* does it do that?'

'Maybe it's because you've got those pipes. Like calls to like.'

My adored Great Treasure was proving to be almost as much a liability as a boon, here in this place of its making. That seemed unfair.

I heard music, then, and cautiously turned back around. Cadence had done I-don't-know-what with the melody, and now the lyre was playing it by itself, its fluid strings rippling in song as an ancient, haunting air filled the echoing library.

I hastily turned my back to it again. Curse the thing, it was almost agonisingly pretty.

'What's this song?' said my father.

'The King's Lament,' said Cadence.

'A song of mourning.'

'Yes.'

It did not sound sufficiently lamenting, to my ear, to qualify as a dirge, but then different cultures do mourn in different ways. This was a hopeful tune, and perhaps that was fitting enough.

Once the song's final strains had died away, though, the lyre lapsed into a thrumming silence, ostensibly unchanged.

Father picked it up and played an experimental note. 'Ineffectual,' he pronounced.

'In what fashion?' said Cadence.

'I want to restore the lyre to its state prior to the events of thirty years ago. Before Ayllindariorana altered its song—'

'Ayllin?!' said Jay and I together.

'*That* woman?' said Mother.

My father looked helplessly at the three of us, nonplussed. 'You've met.'

'She's the one who guided us through to the vault,' I said. 'She's the reason we found you at all.'

'But why would she do that? She hates me.'

'Are you sure?'

'Of course I'm sure. She wanted to install herself as queen, not me.'

'Why?' I said.

He blinked. 'What?'

'Why did she want to be queen so badly?'

'I never asked.' He snorted. 'I hadn't time. They were too busy throwing me out.'

'They who? Was Ayllin one of them?'

'I can't remember.'

Jay and I exchanged a long look. 'Doesn't make sense,' said Jay.

'Not a bit,' I agreed. 'For another thing, if she was willing to go to such lengths to queenify herself, how did the lyre just happen to wind up in your hands instead, Dad? You'd think she would have taken care to eliminate such happenstances.'

'No one can eliminate the effects of chance.'

'True,' I conceded. 'Perhaps it was just an accident.'

'Were you much acquainted with her before that night?' asked Jay.

'No.'

'But she told you her plans anyway.'

'Not before! After, when she was tearing my face off for getting in her way.'

Mother said, 'We need to talk to that woman.'

'She's not popular with you, hm?' said Jay.

'I don't trust her.'

'No,' agreed Jay. 'It would probably be wise not to.'

Mother scowled, and said nothing.

'The lady Ayllindariorana,' said Cadence, 'has often visited this library.'

'To do what?' said Father.

Cadence shrugged. 'She reminisces with the music.'

'She'd like to go back to the old ways, would she? No doubt.'

'You know,' I put in, 'if she wants to be queen so much, and nobody else in this room wants the job, perhaps she should just have it.'

'But she's a liar,' said Father. 'And she cheats.'

'I don't see how that's worse than a king who's ignored his kingdom for the past three decades,' said Mother.

'And it's par for the course for leaders, anyway,' I muttered.

Father threw up his hands. 'Fine. You're right. If it gets me out of this mess, Ayllindariorana for queen.'

'Right.' Mother squared herself up for the task ahead. 'Where do we find Lady Longname?'

But Descant interrupted before anyone could answer. Her squeak of excitement split the air, and she threw a bubble-song up into the air with glee, and caught it again. 'This one, this one!'

Cadence took it, and examined it. 'The Queene's Rapture,' she intoned, in a singsong voice.

'There've been queens!' said Mother. 'Good. You all bang on too much about the kings.'

'I think you mean *queenes*, Mother,' I said. 'With an E.'

She gave me her are-you-crazy stare. 'What?'

I couldn't explain what it was about Cadence's... well, cadence, that had put the thought into my head, so I just said, 'Nothing,' and let it go. At least Jay smirked.

'Ancient faerie queens are always spelt with an E,' he agreed.

'Exactly! Especially the extra magickal ones.'

'Was this an extra magickal one?'

'Indubitably. Just listen to that.' Cadence had set the new song to the lyre, and its dulcet tones now swamped anything else I might have said. I'd heard something before, and recently too, with a similar texture — layers of fae magick woven into the melody — where had it been?

My pipes distracted me, by jumping to join in the singalong. The music deepened, and so did the magick. We all stood bespelled, even the three sprites, until silence returned. When it was over, the lyre seemed to have developed a brighter radiance. Or was that my imagination?

'A little better,' said Father, testing the tone. 'But there is a resistance here.'

Cadence appeared unsurprised.

'Can you go back to being the person you were thirty years ago?' she said, rather cryptically.

'I'd like to,' said Father.

'Would you?'

He hesitated, and thought.

'I would not,' said Mother. 'I was an idiot at that age.' It could be considered ungenerous of her to glower so darkly at my father as she said it.

He spread his hands, his eyebrows going up, the gestures saying as eloquently as words, *not* my *fault!*

'Ahem,' I said. 'Perhaps we could argue about who is to blame for my earthly existence some other time?'

Both parents scowled at me for that, but at least they stopped arguing.

'Lady Smugboots, then,' said Mother. 'Where is she.'

'That song,' said Father. 'We'll take it along.'

Since they spoke at the same time, it took the rest of us a second or two to parse these separate pronouncements.

'Yes, Majesty,' said Cadence.

'I'm not—' began Father, but was soon defeated by Cadence's twinkling, impish smile. 'Right, have it your way.'

'Maestro Ayllindariorana is not in the Halls,' said Euphony. Her eyes went a bit peculiar as she said it, as though she was looking at something very far away — walls notwithstanding.

'We met her in the town,' I said. 'Presumably she went back there after she'd got rid of us.'

'Got rid?' Father's brows snapped together.

'We did get the impression she was glad to see the back of us.'

'Or maybe she was glad to see where we were going,' said Jay.

'One way to find out. To the town?'

I heard a sigh from my mother, a soft one rapidly suppressed. It did then strike me that she was looking grey around the edges again, and her shoulders were slumped.

No wonder, either. Caught up as we'd been in mystery, magic and adventure, we had barely noticed the hours passing. But night must be falling outside, and once it occurred to me to consider the matter, I realised I was ravenously hungry. We'd been running all day, and our last meal had been too many hours ago.

'Perhaps we could rest a little first,' I suggested. 'Dear sprites, do you suppose there is anything resembling sustenance to be had in these parts?'

'There is!' said Euphony. 'In the Queene's Orchard.'

'Does everything around here come with a royal label?'

'It *is* the King's Halls,' Jay pointed out.

'Right. Fine. Which way to the Queene's Orchard, please, Euphony?'

She did not answer, except by an airy laugh. Then, the library dissolved into faerie dust, which swirled around me in a dizzying, twinkling whirlwind.

When it passed, I was standing beneath the arching boughs of a twisted old tree, its gnarled shape casting long shadows on the grass in the dying sunlight. From its boughs hung a multitude of apples. 'Cadence,' I said. 'Descant, Euphony? When we're finished here, I'd really like to talk to you about some exciting employment opportunities at The Society.'

'Hey,' said Father. 'Those are my retainers.'

'So you're the king again now?'

'If you want them, you take the monarchy too.'

'You drive a hard bargain, Father.'

He smirked, and reached out for a plump golden-green apple. But the moment his fingers touched it, it became a wrap sandwich stuffed with what looked like curried chicken, and fell tamely into his palm.

We both looked at it in silence.

'Pork pie!' said Mother, and added gleefully, 'I love pork pie.'

Since Jay had a bag of crisps in one hand and a fat samosa in the other, I judged this to be a highly unusual orchard.

When I reached for an apple of my own, I received a miniature cheese-and-onion quiche and a chunk of Bakewell tart.

'You know what,' I said, clutching my prizes. 'Maybe it wouldn't be that bad to be the queene.'

Mother smirked around her mouthful of pie.

Sustenance and rest restored my mother, to a certain degree, but not enough. The passage of an hour found her slumped beneath a sheltering apple tree, her back against its trunk, eyes shut against the further demands of the day. I watched her for a while, wondering how it was that she had made it through so many hours, even with the restorative I had given her. She sat cradling her injured arm, enduring a species of pain I could only imagine.

Tough lady, my mother.

I'd rummaged through the remains of my minimal equipment, and come up with one more dose of the restorative potion. But, should I give it to mother? She would use it as an excuse to go on, and on, and on, until she collapsed altogether. Potent as it was, I doubted it could bolster her through the demands of, perhaps, a sleepless night filled with frenzied activity.

Would she consent to being left behind? Certainly not.

Would a single night's rest do more for her good than the potion? No, probably not either.

So, then. What was the quickest way to wrap up this bizarre misadventure, the sooner to get my mother out of the kingdom of Yllanfalen and into a hospital, where she presently belonged?

I sat beneath my own tree for the majority of that hour, apart from the rest of our disparate company, and thought.

When at length Jay stood up, peered at me through the twilight, and said: 'We had better find Ayllin before nightfall, no?' I shook my head.

'I have a better idea,' I said.

'Uh oh.' Jay took two steps back.

I smiled briefly. 'I don't think you're going to like it all that much.'

He folded his arms, squared his shoulders, and lifted his chin. 'Right. Hit me with it.'

'We're throwing a party.'

'A what.'

'Like the one my esteemed parents attended thirty years ago. Forget finding Ayllin — let her find us, together with the rest of the kingdom, when they all show up for the festival.'

'It's not a festival day, is it?'

'The king is going to declare a new one.' I beamed at my father. 'Right now.'

17

'Your mother can't withstand a wild night like that,' hissed Jay to me, having drawn closer to me and farther away from the mother in question.

'She doesn't need to do much. We put her in a comfy chair, ply her with victuals, let her sleep through it if she wants.'

'Ves, will you please *think* about something or someone other than the mission.'

'I am! What else are we going to do with my mother? She won't be left out, she won't be sent for treatment until this is all over, and she won't be fit and healthy until she's had at least a week's rest and care. We need to wrap this up tonight, and this is the best way I can think of to do it.'

Jay nodded. 'All right, I can't fault that logic, as far as it goes. But what are we doing with this party?'

I cleared my throat. 'Dad will kick off the festival. I'm sure there are ways to make a suitably public show of it, get everybody here. Right, your majesty?'

My father rolled his eyes towards the sky. 'Doubtless, but—'

'Ayllin will be here with the rest. We find her, ask her what she did to alter the lyre's song, get her to change it back, and then let nature take its course. Pass the lyre around, spend the rest of the evening in wine and song, and at some point it will choose a new monarch. Right? And then we all go home and sleep for a week. Especially Mum.'

'Just "get her" to uncorrupt the lyre?' said Mother. 'Right! I'm sure there can be no possible objection to that.'

I shrugged. 'If it's a choice between that, or going on forever without a leader, I hope she'll see sense. And it could be her chance to take the throne at last, if she still wants it.'

'You're forgetting something,' said my father. 'They hate me.'

'The Yllanfalen?'

'Yes. They threw me out, rather than accept me as king. What makes you think they'll all come blithely party with me now?'

'They threw you out, but you are still the king. Aren't you?'

'I... yes.'

'I think they couldn't have turfed you out if you hadn't let them. You let them because you did not want the role. Well, now you can pass it on.'

'But—'

'Come on, Dad. We can't do this without you.'

Father scowled in my mother's general direction. 'Is she always like this?'

'Yes,' said Jay.

'And you haven't gone insane yet?'

'It gets things done.'

'Being insane?'

Jay blinked. 'Well... that, too.'

Father sighed, and directed his attention towards the three sprites, whose only contribution to the debate thus far had been suppressed squeaks of excitement from Euphony. 'Will the sprites assist me?'

'Yes, Majesty!' said Cadence, in a ringing voice.

'I will never get used to that,' muttered Father.

I got up from under my tree. 'Fortunately, you won't have to. Let's get started. The sooner we're finished raving, the sooner we can sleep.'

IT WAS THE SPRITES who carried word of the revelry.

Everything began in the throne room of the King's Halls, as was fitting. This space we had never glimpsed before, or I'd have certainly remembered, for the chamber was improbably enormous, and sumptuously decorated, even by the standards of the Yllanfalen. Chandeliers as big as my car were suspended from the ceiling, and when Euphony glided, chortling, up to greet them they burst into life, casting a vibrant, sunny glow over the hall. In that light we saw: great, lush hangings covering the walls, worked in silk and velvet and gilded thread, and depicting myriad mythical beasts; a floor of polished... something, that shone as silver as the chandeliers shone gold; long, long windows, arched and ornamented, beyond which the velvet-black night lay waiting; and a banqueting table, fully thirty feet long, already set with all the ornate silverware one might need for a kingdom-sized party.

Father beheld all this magnificence in silence, and gave only a weary sigh. Mother's response was not much more enthusiastic.

Jay and I, though, were entranced. Jay especially, once he saw that, at the far-distant end of the throne room — situated not far from the throne itself, a confection of mist-whorled glass and cushions of green-and-gold moss — sat a grand piano, or something that closely resembled a piano. It had none of the mirror-polished, black elegance of a typical example from our world; instead it looked wrought from silver, or similar, its surfaces frosted over and a-twinkle with... ice? But its shape was familiar enough, and its bright white keys begged to be played.

Jay began to drift that way.

'Well,' said Father, wearily. 'Let's begin.'

'How?' said Mother.

'With music. Out here, it *always* begins with music.'

Jay reached the piano, and sat down upon the silvery-frosted stool before it. He made an incongruous sight: clad in his adored black leather jacket, and with his short, dark, eminently modern hair, seated upon azure velvet stitched with silver and playing a piano from which magick dripped like melting ice.

But when he began to play, I realised at once why the Queene's Rapture had struck a familiar chord with me. The melody Jay's clever fingers were drawing forth was the same as he had once played upon the spinet in Millie Makepeace's parlour, and it shimmered and twinkled like faerie bells.

Father raised his brows at me.

'I don't know,' I said. Life had been busy. I'd forgotten to ask Jay about it.

'Unusual chap, I think,' said Father.

I was beginning to get an inkling of that myself.

The sprites had been busy. The piano was not the only instrument in the throne room, I soon saw: what I had previously taken for carvings and ornaments proved to be lutes and pipes and lyres, and one by one the sprites were bringing them into melodious life.

Actually, I take that back. They *were* carvings. I watched, open-mouthed, as Descant soared up the length of a grand pilaster set against one wall, reaching out with her small hands to touch and touch and touch. Everywhere her fingers brushed the stone, an inert sculpture leapt free of the pillar, transformed at a stroke into gleaming metal or polished wood, and began to play. Jay had finished his gossamer tune and taken up the Queene's Rapture instead, and the sprites had every harp and dulcimer and flute playing along.

The effect was both deafening and rhapsodic. Indeed, one may even say... rapturous.

Mum made a sound that was half sigh, half groan, and folded into a chair at the table. I took the opportunity to hand her my last dose of potion, pleased to note that the empty silverware was rapidly filling up with delectable feast-goods under Cadence's capable attention.

'Drink,' I said to Mother. 'But try not to overdo it. It's borrowed strength these things give you. You'll pay for it later.'

Mother didn't even try to argue, which told me all I needed to know about how exhausted she was. She drank off the potion in one swallow, blotted her lips on her sleeve, and said grimly: 'I'll be fine.'

'Uh huh.'

She waved me off. 'Don't forget to play later.'

'I haven't the smallest desire to play that lyre, Mother.'

'You know you do. Your eyes say otherwise, every time you look at the thing.'

'That's not my fault.'

'Nope.' She grinned. 'It's your destiny.'

'I don't believe in destiny, and neither do you.'

'Maybe I do, now.'

I decided we were done with the conversation, and walked away.

At once I observed that Father had done something highly out of character for him.

He'd made himself comfy on the Throne of the Yllan-falen.

He actually looked pretty good up there, I have to say. Tall, grey of hair and beard, noble; his face was set in res-olute lines, and he looked ready to rule.

Appearances can be so deceptive.

I'd lost sight of the sprites. As far as I could tell, they were no longer in the throne room. That, perhaps, was because they'd gone out to wake up the kingdom and spread the party news, for soon afterwards the people of Yllanfalen began to arrive.

They ventured in tentatively, at first, gazing upon the throne room's revived splendours in wary astonishment. And well they might, considering all this had lain untouched for decades.

But, it does not take much to coax the Yllanfalen into making merry, for they soon forgot their worries, and began snatching up flutes and harps from the walls, and delicacies from the table.

Until, that is, they caught sight of my father, seated in solitary majesty upon his throne. A crowd quickly developed at that end of the throne room, and grew larger and larger as more people arrived. These fae lords and ladies even managed to cluster decorously, for there was no pushing or shoving, no noise, no unseemly chaos. They stared, and they talked, and they waited, though any fool could see that they were not pleased.

My father stared them all down, every inch a king, and I wondered where he had been hiding that quality. In his lap, the moonsilver lyre glimmered with promise, and I realised *that* was as much the focus of the Yllanfalen's attention as the king himself.

In fact, I began to feel they might have cheerfully dispensed with my father's presence altogether — provided he left the lyre.

This did not quite fit with the narrative that the Yllan-falen had themselves rejected the lyre. Perhaps they had not. But then, if they had wanted it back, why hadn't they taken it out of the water?

Time to talk to Ayllin.

I wasted ten minutes or so weaving through the increasingly crowded throne room, looking for Ayllin with my own eyes. By the end of it, I judged I had personally scrutinised about a hundred people at best, and how many thousands were by now thronging the King's Halls? Better plan required.

Briefly I considered asking my father to call her up, but discarded the notion. This was not a conversation to be held in public.

The alternative, then? The sprites could find her in no time, no doubt. But where were they?

A recent memory popped into my head. *Syllphyllan,* the woman at the music shop had said. *A favourite with gardeners and orchard-tenders, as the sprites adore it.*

All right, then.

I snatched up the sheaf of music I'd received only a few hours ago, and sorted hastily through until I found *Syllphyllan.* Would Cadence, Euphony or Descant — or any of their sisters, as I imagined there must be more — hear a note of it over the tumult? Maybe not, but it was worth a try.

Out came my pipes. The first few phrases emerged awkwardly from the silvery flute, for my talent for sight-reading isn't what it should be. But I soon got into the flow, doing my best to tune out the roar of faerie music around me. I probably got half of it wrong; I couldn't even hear what I was playing.

Then again, if I got half wrong, then I got half right, too. I was nearing the end of the song when a voice whispered in my ear.

'Who plays *Syllphyllan* on the King's Pipes?'

I spun, to find Euphony had come up behind me... no, it was not Euphony. Another sprite, paler and smaller still, hovered by my shoulder. She wore a gauzy dress of heathery gossamer, and a hat of leaves crowned her tumble of wispy hair; more a sprite by appearance than Cadence, with her lumpy knitted drape.

'I wanted to ask your help,' I said.

'There are no orchards here,' the sprite pointed out. 'No hedgerows, no herb gardens, no flowers, no fields, no—'

'Yes, I know,' I interrupted, for fear she would go on until she had named every possible growing thing. 'It isn't gardening I need help with.'

'But you played *Syllphyllan* on—'

'The King's Pipes. It was the best I had. I am actually looking for someone.'

A cloud of displeasure descended upon her small face. 'Then you should have played a song of seeking.'

'I am sorry. I would have, if I knew one. Will you help me? It's important work for the king.'

'If it is the king you seek, he is there.' She pointed a slender finger in my father's direction.

'Yes, but I don't need him at the moment. The woman I want is called Ayllin.'

'I do not know that name.'

Ohgods. That's right, we had dubbed her *Ayllin* ourselves, for her whole name was... difficult.

'Ayllindariana,' I tried.

The sprite shook her head.

'Ayllindarinda?'

'No.'

'Ayllindariolonda?'

The sprite folded her arms, and glared at me. 'There is no such person.'

Giddy gods, I'd never get it right. I tried a few more variations, with no more success; but just as my not-so-obliging sprite was about to give up on me and wing away, another voice said: 'Is it Ayllindariorana you seek?'

'Yes!' I shouted. 'That was it!'

And Ayllindariorana herself emerged from the crowd, looking none too pleased. I suppose if someone mangled my name the way I'd just wrecked hers, I would be none too pleased either. 'Can I help you with something?' she said icily.

'Actually, yes,' I said. 'Just one or two little things.'

18

'It's about the lyre,' I said to Ayllin.

'I could have guessed that much,' she replied. Her eyes strayed to my father, still seated upon his throne, with the moonsilver lyre in his lap. I tried to read her expression, but failed; she was impassive, after an icy fashion.

'Can you fix it?'

Her gaze returned to me. 'Fix it?'

'Yes.'

'Is it broken?'

'Um. My father's presence on that throne says it is.'

To my surprise (and discomfort), she smiled at that with genuine amusement. 'Perhaps he is not the only one who has drawn such a conclusion,' she said. 'But he's no less wrong for it.'

'I... don't understand.'

'How did you get it back?'

'The lyre?'

'*Yes,* the lyre. What is it doing here?'

'We retrieved it from the water, obviously.'

'We?'

'Yes. You knew that was the goal — you helped us. So why do you ask?'

Her lips pursed. 'I have helped many on that particular quest. I had no reason to imagine you would be successful, but it is always worth another try.'

'So you *wanted* the lyre back? My father said—'

'Your father appears to be spectacularly misinformed,' she said, betraying a trace of irritation. 'Which ought not to surprise us, considering he has spent a mere matter of hours among his people.'

'*His* people threw him out. Is that not the case?

'His people required a period of adjustment, to adapt to so much change. If he had stayed—'

'If? Did the Yllanfalen throw him out, or did they not?'

'Yes, but—'

'And the lyre with him.'

'There was anger. It was my fault. I mishandled the matter.'

'So I heard.' I folded my arms, and did my best to stare the lady out of countenance. I do not much enjoy being so thoroughly confused. 'The lyre was meant to choose you, no? But strayed into my father's hands by accident. Mishandled indeed.'

'Accident? It would be impossible to control the course of that lyre on festival night. It takes its own course, and chooses who it will. I had hoped it would choose me, but it did not.'

'Hoped! So you did not manipulate its song? You didn't fix it up to pick whoever got hold of it next?'

'Is that what our precious king thinks?'

'He is quite convinced of it.'

'Well. He's modest enough, I will give him that.' A faint smile ghosted over her face. 'He is still wrong. Supposing it were possible to impose such a course upon that lyre, and I highly doubt it: no Yllanfalen could be so crude. Don't you see? It is not enough simply to *have* a monarch, any monarch. It must be the right one for the era. One who can be... what we need.'

'And what did you need, thirty years ago?'

'Change.' She was not laughing now. 'We had grown set in our ways. Too hidden from the outside world, too closed to everything that is not tradition. It is a poor course for any culture, is it not? Look at the wider world now. So many kingdoms, so many cultures, have faded away forever — and it's my belief they exacerbated their down troubles by their very efforts to mitigate them. Closing one's doors to progress achieves nothing but stagnation and decay. We did not want that for the Yllanfalen.'

'We?'

'Our former queen, and many others, including myself. Did you never ask your father why he was here that night?'

'No... nor my mother either.'

'That was no accident. It was our choice to throw open the doors, to invite everyone who might feel some affinity with us and our ways. And if the lyre chose outside of our own people: perhaps that would be right.'

'But your own people were not quite so happy with this as you'd hoped.'

'No. Neither, crucially, was your father. And that is one thing we did not count on: the lyre must choose a monarch, but the monarch must also choose themselves. Your father did not.'

I took a moment to think, and wrap my head around Ayllin's words. The ground was shifting under me so fast, I could barely keep up. 'Right. But, wait. I see that it went wrong, and — what, the doors were closed again anyway?'

'With greater emphasis than before,' said Ayllin, with a wry smile.

'Talk about unintended consequences.'

'Yes. Rather what I meant, when I said that one's best efforts to mend a problem can sometimes deepen it.'

'But why then did you never try again? Why leave the lyre languishing at the bottom of a pool for thirty years?'

'Oh, we tried. And we encountered a new problem: over some things, the monarch's will holds total sway. One such, of course, is the lyre.'

'Ohgods.' I thought back to my doomed attempt to swipe that other set of skysilver pipes off the effigy of King Evelaern. 'That's why we couldn't get the pipes.'

'You tried, did you? Many have tried before you. And many tried to remove the lyre, too, with no more success. The bottom of the pool was its appointed place, as far as our king was concerned. Only he could reverse that command, and take it out again.'

My breath stopped, for a long, agonising moment, as my mind turned a few unhappy somersaults.

'What?' said Ayllin. 'What is it?'

'Um,' I croaked. 'Only the king...?'

'So it seems, for none other has succeeded.'

'And... and, um, do you *have* to play the lyre in order to be chosen as monarch?'

'That is how it has always been done.'

'But you wanted change.' I had to laugh, though the sound had more despair in it than mirth.

Ayllin's eyes widened. 'It... it *was* the king who retrieved the lyre, wasn't it?'

'No.'

'Was it... you?'

'No.'

I saw dismay in her face. 'Was it that handsome fellow you travel with? He plays the ancient airs like no one I've heard.'

My eyebrows rose. 'Jay? No.'

Her face fell. 'Then it was—'

'That lady. Yep.' My mother was on the approach, elbowing people aside as she stomped and pushed her way through the crowd. She looked in as good a mood as a day of disasters and constant pain was likely to produce, and fixed both of us with a forbidding scowl.

'Cordelia,' she growled. 'These sprites will not leave me alone.'

Looking behind her, I saw Cadence, Euphony, and Descant, together with a few unfamiliar ones. How many more might be hovering invisibly around her?

Ayllin gave a great sigh, and I detected a brief roll of her eyes heavenwards. Then, to my surprise and my mother's obvious disgust, she performed a graceful curtsey and said: 'They are eager to greet you, Majesty, as am I. Welcome.'

Mother stared. 'You appear to be mistaking me for my... for that man.' She waved her stump in Dad's general direction.

'I think not.'

'Don't be absurd.' Mother turned her shoulder to Ayllin, and frowned darkly at me. 'I begin to think you were right. I'd be glad of some rest. Can we go? I can't get that boy to stop playing the piano either.'

A fine concession from my mother; it told me that she was suffering, if her pallid face and weary gait had not been enough. 'I don't think that's going to be possible now, Mother. Though if you want rest, you've only to say so, and your people will no doubt provide you with everything you could want.'

'This isn't an amusing joke, Cordelia.'

'No. No, it really isn't.'

'Then take me home. I am sure the selection of a new leader can go on without us.'

'It's already happened.'

The sprites, indeed, were backing us up with coaxing professions of joy, devotion and concern, together with assorted requests and petitions. My mother ignored all of it.

'The thing is, Mother,' I said, interrupting her next diatribe. 'You shouldn't have been able to take the lyre out of the pool at all.'

'Shouldn't? But it was the easiest thing in the world. I just reached in and...' She trailed off.

I mustered a faint smile. 'It seems you weren't the only one to try that. You were the only one to succeed, though.'

'No.' Mother stared at me with something like anguish. 'It was meant to be *you*. I took the lyre for you!'

'Nonetheless.'

'But you wanted it, Cordelia. Anyone could see that, whenever you looked at it—'

'I may lust after that lyre, but not the trappings that go with it. Besides, Mother, you miss the point. It's not about wanting the lyre. It's about the lyre wanting *you*.'

'Why would it want me?!'

'Good question. Are you going to argue about it all night?'

'Or,' Ayllin put in, 'run away from us, like the last one?'

'What makes you think your damned xenophobic people will want me any more than they wanted Tom?'

'Tom's accession was thirty years ago. Change touches us all, in the end.'

'There's one way to be certain about this,' I said. 'Ayllin, you must know that my mother has scarcely a drop of musical talent in her.'

Ayllin's lips quirked. 'Well, that is certainly... new.'

'Quite. So, let's go talk to Dad.' I took hold of Mother Dearest and plunged into the crowd, heading for the throne. I'd expected to spend a few minutes pushing and shoving in order to reach it, but Mother — ever her impatient self, and now infinitely weary to boot — barked, 'Oh for goodness' sake, just step aside!'

And they did. A clear corridor opened up for us through the throng of people, giving us an unimpeded view of the throne.

Mother gaped. Those who'd so obligingly cleared space for us looked scarcely less surprised.

I grinned. 'Oh, life never gets any less bizarre, does it?'

Jay stepped into view, flanking my father's right hand. He'd abandoned the piano at last, apparently in favour of a little lap-harp, which he cradled in both hands. A wooden flute hung around his neck. 'What's going on?' he said.

'We're about to witness a coronation,' I told him. 'Of sorts.'

He looked aghast. 'Ves, no. You can't let yourself be pushed into this.'

I flashed him a swift smile. 'Don't panic. It isn't me.'

His eyes went from me, to Mother, to Ayllin, and settled on the latter.

'Nope, wrong again. Dad? Can we have that lyre a minute?'

My father, for all his complaints, exhibited a trace of reluctance as he held out the lyre. I wondered what it had cost him to throw it away in the first place, for all that he did not want the responsibilities it conferred.

But he was holding it out to me; even he could not grasp the truth without assistance. I stepped aside, and ushered Mother forward.

'Just give it a quick go, Mum. If you're right and this is an absurd joke, you'll soon prove it.'

Mother glowered at me, but snatched up the lyre with her good hand. There followed an ungainly fumble, for a one-handed lyre player will always find herself at a disadvantage.

My father's eyes sparked with amusement. 'You'll need to sit down,' he said, and rose from his own seat upon the throne. 'Why don't you try this one?'

Muttering something about conspiracies, Mother plunked herself down on the throne and settled the lyre in her lap.

And the matter was promptly settled, for once she'd set her good hand to the strings, her fingers began to move as though she had played the lyre since the cradle, and what poured forth was the most heavenly, ambrosial melody I could ever remember hearing. She even outdid Jay's playing; her sudden talent far exceeded mine.

I gave up a polite round of applause. 'Congratulations, Father. You're liberated.'

And my father, wretch that he was, promptly went off into a gale of helpless laughter.

19

It was too cruel to abandon my mother to her new role among the Yllanfalen straight away, though I was sorely tempted, for her sudden accession to rank and privilege had only soured her temper further. But Jay and I agreed to stay for a day or two, to see that she received suitable care.

We needn't have been concerned. The sprites may have treated my father with indifference, but for some reason they adored my mother. They flocked around her, plied her with curatives and pillows and sweetmeats and every good thing, and played her lullabies until she fell asleep (or hurled her pillows at their heads, which she tried once and never attempted again, for the immediate and predictable result was a mass pillow fight).

Ayllin conducted her, very late that night, to a sumptuous suite of rooms near the top of the King's Halls (henceforth to be termed the Queen's Halls, no doubt). Whereupon, she disappeared into the depths of the largest, most ornate bed I have ever seen, and for the next two days thereafter spent little time awake.

My father was not disposed to await her waking. He consented to spend a night among the Yllanfalen, but no more, for bright and early the next morning he appeared in the Queen's Breakfast Parlour (where Jay and I were dining in mother's place) with the brisk air of a man desirous of immediate departure.

'She'll do fine,' he told me, then hesitated. 'Won't she?'

'Once she's got used to the idea. You haven't seen Delia when she's got a project in hand. The Yllanfalen won't know what hit them.'

'My commiserations to the Yllanfalen.'

I smiled. 'No, I think this is just what Ayllin and the rest were hoping for. It might take them a while to get used to my mother's methods, but she'll get the job done.'

'And what's the job?'

'Overhaul?' I shrugged. 'If they want to survive, well, no one survives the slings and arrows of outrageous fortune like my mother.'

'With or without a full set of hands.'

'You see my point.'

He smiled, faint and wintry. 'Maybe the lyre got it right, the second time.'

'It must've seen some qualities in you, Dad.'

'Goodness knows what they were. Anyway, I depart.' He nodded at Jay in friendly enough fashion, who nodded back, and added a wave. 'Take care of Cordelia,' said Dad.

'It's Ves,' I said.

Jay grinned at me. 'I will, sir, but you should have realised by now: Ves is more of a chip off her mother's block than she likes to think.'

'I don't know what that is supposed to mean,' I said, with a flinty look.

He pointed a chunk of fresh bread at my face. 'That, right there.'

I composed my features into an expression of sunny serenity. 'I have no idea what you're talking about.'

Dad hesitated. In fact, he positively dithered. 'Cordelia—' he began.

'Ves.'

'Ves, then.' He dithered some more, then gave up whatever the point might have been, and shook his head. 'It was good to meet you.'

'Mm. You too.' I watched as he walked away, dithering a bit myself.

Jay was busy buttering another roll. He said, without looking at me, 'You'll regret it if you don't.'

'Curse it.' I launched myself out of my chair and ran to the door, just as my father disappeared from view. 'Dad?'

He returned. 'Yes?'

'Erm. Sprites?' I said, groping at thin air. 'Anybody got a thing to write with?'

'A thing?' said Cadence in my ear, though without troubling to manifest.

'Pen, pencil, quill, tomato juice, fresh blood— ah! Perfect, thank you.' An exquisite pen of coiled silver leaves appeared in front of my nose, together with a miniature scroll. When I set pen to paper, a shimmering silvery ink poured forth. Never have my name and phone number looked more magnificent.

I handed the results to Tom. 'In case you feel more like being a dad than being a king.'

'It's possible,' he said, and tucked the paper into his trouser pocket. 'I couldn't have been less interested in being a king.' He stooped to give me the briefest peck on the cheek, and then he was gone.

I wandered back to Jay, feeling vaguely dissatisfied with this response. 'Does that mean he does or doesn't want to be my idol, role model and hero?'

'I don't wish to insult your father, but I think he's a tiny bit of a coward,' said Jay. 'It's my belief he'll square up to the idea, though, given a little time.'

I leaned my cheek in one hand, and toyed with a bit of fruit left on my plate (some unidentifiable thing resembling a peach crossed with a cherry). 'I'm not sure I want a coward for a hero.'

'You've courage enough for both of you. Cut him some slack.'

'Is your father a hero?'

'Every inch of him.' Jay said this with pride, but it was mixed with something wry and rueful. 'I'll introduce you sometime.'

I perked up at that. If Jay wanted to present me to his heroes, maybe I wasn't doing a bad job of being Ves after all.

Jay smirked at me, and added, 'I'd better make sure they put on a spread fit for a princess.'

'*Don't* call me that.'

'Why not? You're the descendant of a king and a queen.'

'My father was king in name only, and doesn't count. Anyway, it's not hereditary around here, however much Mum might have wished otherwise.'

'I wonder why she wanted that for you.'

'Mum was always good at that. Long periods of neglect, then some peculiar attack of remorse and she'd make some big gesture to make up for it.'

'This was a pretty big gesture.'

'Six years was a pretty long silence.'

He conceded the point with a nod. 'So what's next for us, if it isn't royalty and privilege?'

I went to chew a fingernail, and stopped myself in the nick of time. 'I want to contact the Court at Mandridore, see if there's news about Torvaston's book. Or that box of junk we picked up.'

'Junk?' Jay spluttered. 'The jewels on that scroll case alone could buy my parents' house.'

'I meant junk in the sense of random. A fork? A snuff box? What does it all mean?'

'Maybe nothing. I imagine even kings accumulate clutter.'

'Don't ruin my dreams.'

'Sorry.' He grinned. 'I'm sure it's the Enchanted Fork of Magick and Wonder.'

'Doubtless. And the Snuff Box of Mystery and Dreams.'

'With a naked lady on the lid.'

'It wasn't a— no, never mind.'

'Wise choice.'

After a couple of days of kicking our heels in the Queen's Halls, hobnobbing with the sprites (mostly me), and playing hauntingly beautiful music on every instrument we could lay our hands on (mostly Jay), we grew bored.

Actually, that was mostly me, too.

I announced that my mother clearly had no need of us, and set forth to bid her a firm goodbye.

I found her reclining in a state of near unconsciousness in her boudoir of pillows, attended by three hovering sprites. Her eyes opened when she saw me. 'Cordelia.'

'Mother. We're off.' I bent to kiss her cheek.

'Wait.' She sat up, wincing. 'The— the lyre. Where is it.'

'Lying on your throne. Do you mean to retrieve those pipes, by the by?'

'Nope. We don't need 'em. Nor the lyre either, for now. Take it.'

My feelings about that idea could only be expressed by my backing away, very quickly. 'No. I'm not touching it.'

'Get Jay to take it, then.'

'I don't think he wants to touch it either.'

She snorted. 'One of you will have to.'

'Have to?'

'I promised Milady.'

'A few things have changed since then.'

'A promise is a promise. Take it.'

'Milady wouldn't choose to divest the new Queen of the Yllanfalen of her sacred instrument—'

'*Take it.*' Mother was growing agitated, which in her case meant aggressive. 'I promised her. She made me promise.'

'Made you?' I echoed numbly. 'No one can make you do anything, Mother.'

'Except for Milady. Cordelia, the sole reason you were sent out here was to get that lyre. You won't be popular if you go back without it.'

'Why does she want it so badly?'

Mother wheezed, which I realised was meant to be a laugh. 'She told me all about her plans in exhaustive detail, naturally. After that, we had a pyjama party and braided each other's hair.'

'I see your point.'

'Mm.'

'I'm still not touching it.'

'Then I hope your man Jay's braver than you.'

'He's not my— I'm not a coward!'

Mother just looked at me.

'*Fine,* we'll take it. But what does the damned thing even do, besides install monarchs on that shiny throne down there?'

'I don't know, quite, but...' Mother lapsed into thought for a moment. 'It has an unusual line on the past, I think.'

'What does that mean?'

'I can sense bits and pieces of a location's past, to a certain degree. I told you that. When I had that lyre in my hands...' She was growing tired with the effort of talking, and fell silent for a moment. 'Whoosh,' she finished feebly, making a something-exploding gesture with her good hand.

If Mother was right about that, I began to get an inkling as to why Milady wanted to borrow it. 'It would make sense,' I suggested. 'It is an instrument of history and tradition.'

'Until lately.' Mother's eyes crinkled in a tired smile.

'Change comes to us all. But why aren't we borrowing you as well as the lyre, in that case? Your ability there isn't too common.'

'Milady probably has someone for that.'

Could be so. The Society employed quite a lot of people, and Milady made a point of collecting the rarer talents.

Mother's eyes closed again. I watched her for a little while, trying to convince myself that her pallor was fading. She looked terribly weak, and somehow... forlorn, adrift within that enormous bed by herself.

Her eyes snapped open. 'Weren't you going?'

'Right. Sorry. Bye, Mum.'

'IT IS A TRULY remarkable thing,' said Milady upon the following morrow.

Jay and I were at the top of her tower, comfortably seated in chairs of House's providing. The lyre occupied a plinth before us; that, too, had been spun out of nothing by our beloved House, and it was of fitting beauty: silver studded with amethysts, and attractively carved. House had style. The moonsilver lyre sat there sparkling dreamily in the sun, its strings peacefully flowing, emitting a faint, fae melody to tease our ears.

I'd taken it up, at first. Jay had taken one look at my eyes, and swiftly swiped it off me.

'Nope, nope, nope,' he'd said. 'Bad idea.'

I'd studied him carefully for some minutes afterwards, but he showed no signs of developing the same peculiar symptoms as I did.

And lo, Jay became our designated lyre-carrier.

'It's one of the oldest Great Treasures I have seen, or even heard of,' Milady continued, in a voice of uncharacteristic enthusiasm. 'To think that it has been lying in a pond these thirty years!'

'I can only apologise for my father,' I said.

Milady said, more gravely: 'I must apologise, Ves. I had no idea the venture would prove so... personally significant for you.'

'Except that it began with my mother.'

'Delia gave me no reason to imagine you were so completely out of touch.'

'Would you have chosen differently, if you had known some of these things?'

When Milady decided to be open and honest, she really did it properly. 'No,' she said.

'Shall we move on from the apologies, then? Why have we just retrieved this lyre?'

'I believe it may be of use to us in the matter of Farringale, and perhaps the fifth Britain. If the reports of its talents are true, much may be learned. It goes to Orlando's department at once, and I have hopes of hearing something shortly.'

'Orlando? Why?' He was our inventor. His specialty was new stuff, not dusty old artefacts.

'Because nobody understands the inner workings of enchantments better than he, and his associates. How do you suppose he produces such high quality products? His creations are not produced out of thin air. He has studied a vast number of existing artefacts and treasures.'

'Right. Has there been any word from the Court?'

'Little of relevance, yet. Torvaston's book is being translated and studied as we speak, though it has yet to shed any light on those objects you retrieved along with it.'

My heart sank a little. I'd hoped to have something new to dive into as soon as we returned.

Perhaps Jay had, too, for he said: 'What would you like for us to do next, then?'

'You are free to take some time off, if you'd like.'

Time off? My mind went blank at the prospect. When was the last time I'd had more than, say, half a weekend of free time?

'Great,' said Jay, rising from his chair. 'Because it's Anaya's birthday, and I'm late.'

'Convey my greetings to your family, Jay,' said Milady.

'Absolutely, ma'am.' Jay bowed.

'Who's Anaya?' I asked as he passed me.

'My sister.'

'How many sisters do you have?'

'Three. I'll see you in a couple of days, all right?' He smiled at me, and left.

A couple of days. I watched the door close on his retreating back.

'Can I stay here?' I asked, trying not to sound plaintive.

Milady hesitated. Probably she should say no.

'Yes, Ves,' she said instead. 'It has been a difficult week for you, hasn't it?'

'I'm fine.'

'Of course. There's chocolate in the pot. And on this occasion, you will find your pot on Valerie's desk.'

I FOUND TWO POTS on Val's desk, in fact, and some more joys besides. Enthroned atop the expansive surface lay my favourite book in the world: dear Mauf, his purple covers gleaming. And curled atop Mauf was a tufty bundle of yellow fur, sound asleep.

Val was deep in a book, of course; I rarely saw her in any other state. She did not immediately look up as I trailed into the library, so I sat in the chair opposite and laid my cheek against Robin Goodfellow's soft fur.

'Bad week, hm?' said Val.

'Mmpf,' I said.

She closed her book, handling it with tender care. 'The Baron left those for you. He's off on some kind of diplomatic mission, and said you'd probably want them.'

'So I do.' I sat up and poured chocolate.

'Is that for me?' said Val, pointing at the second pot.

'I expect so. Milady sent me down here.'

'Why?'

'No idea. Actually, she didn't send me so much as put my chocolate down here as bait.'

'I don't have much for you to do.'

'It's okay. Apparently I am having "time off".'

Valerie blinked. 'Oh.'

I gulped chocolate.

Valerie watched me with her steady dark eyes, and nodded slowly. 'You'd better tell me about it, hadn't you.'

'Do you want to hear about it?'

'I don't know. Do I?'

I began, wretchedly, to laugh. 'It makes the most farcical story. You may not believe me.'

Val took a swallow of chocolate, and grinned. 'I like farce. Hit me with it.'

And I did.

A WEEK DRIFTED BY, only some of which I spent at Home. After a day or two of basking in House's familiar comforts, I felt obliged to remove to the Scarlet Courtyard, and bask in Mrs. Amberstone's comforts instead (which, to be fair, are not insignificant). Jay had leave to remain with his family for much of it, which was doubtless good for him. I tried to recall if he'd managed to have more than an afternoon off since he'd joined the Society, and concluded possibly not. Good sport, Jay. It would be a shame to burn him out.

The problem with a lifestyle like ours is, you forget what to do with free time. I lounged; I chatted with Val; I caught up on a bit of walking, and a bit of reading. There was cake, which I ate listlessly.

I slept too much.

No doubt this was good for me, too, for when a summons to Milady's tower materialised some eight or nine days later, *enthusiasm* couldn't begin to cover my feelings.

I was back at Home and at the top of the tower within an hour.

'Welcome, Ves,' said Milady as I ventured in. An elegant chair had been placed for me, facing the centre of the room, where manifested the faint sparkle in the air that was all one ever saw of Milady. The suggestion of a second chair occupied a spot nearby, an intangible outline; House had got halfway through conjuring another, and paused.

'Good morning, Milady,' I said with my usual curtsey, and took the solid chair.

'I trust you are well?'

'Yes,' I said. 'If a little bored.'

The sparkle intensified: amusement. 'You ought to have time off more often,' she said. 'There are laws about that sort of thing.'

I tried to feel as though that would be a nice idea. 'What would I do with it?'

'Jay, for example, has been—'

'Visiting his family.'

Milady acknowledged the justice of my unspoken objection with a polite silence. 'Relations with your mother are...?'

'Still peculiar. Likely to become more so, now that someone's been idiot enough to give her free rein to boss everyone around.'

'Perhaps she will benefit from a suitable outlet for that side of her personality.'

'I am unlikely to see anything of it, if she does.'

'Very well.' I braced myself for questions about my father, but Milady permitted the subject to drop. 'I would have spoken to you yesterday, but we await Jay—'

'Here,' said Jay, and the door opened smartly to admit him. He smiled at me, looking bright-eyed, glowing with health and very happy indeed.

'Good week?' I said, returning the smile.

'Splendid. The girls are doing well. Dev's up to his eyeballs in exams, but he'll fly through them; nobody's worried about that except him. And I met—' He stopped abruptly, and cast me a look I found it impossible to interpret. 'It was a good week,' he finished, and turned away his eyes.

The second chair took solid shape, and Jay sank into it. 'I brought Indira back, ma'am. She's on her way to Orlando.'

'I know. Thank you, Jay.'

He grinned. 'Of course you do.'

'I have a new assignment for you both,' she said. 'If you are ready to continue?'

'Perfectly,' I said.

'Absolutely,' said Jay.

'Excellent. I have had word from Mandridore regarding those books you secured from Farringale. They are not yet fully deciphered, and there is some disagreement as to the precise import of some parts. However, there appears to be some support for the hypothesis you formulated on that occasion: namely the links between magickal creatures such as griffins, and magickal surges.'

'So they *are* linked,' I said, with a glow of satisfaction.

'There appears to be some support for the idea,' Milady repeated, which meant: *maybe, but don't get carried away.* 'Certainly it appears that the causal relationships here may have been misinterpreted. Are griffins drawn to areas of excess magick, or do certain areas become concentrated sources of magick because of their griffin population?'

'Maybe some of both,' Jay suggested.

'Yes; a symbiosis, which can on occasion get out of hand. That is possible, maybe even likely. And if this is the case, then the gradual decline of magick in Britain can be partly attributed to the commensurate decline in such creatures as griffins.

'So: what can be done about this?'

All sorts of possibilities popped into my mind, one thought chief amongst them. 'Had they begun to realise this in Torvaston's day?'

'Yes,' said Milady. 'His books indicate that the notion had occurred to the Court's scholars. Of course, there is no real consensus among academics as to when the decline truly began, or how far back it can be traced; reports are conflicting, and conclusions differ widely. But if Torvaston and Hrruna knew of it, then that casts a different light on some things.'

'Such as what they were doing with Farringale's griffin population,' I said. 'Perhaps I was wrong. Perhaps Torvaston wasn't magick-drunk and addicted. Maybe he was... trying to help.'

'Both,' said Milady. 'Possibly the former came about as a result of the latter, at least in part. His books seem to indicate it.'

Which made him a rather tragic figure after all, if it was true.

'What was he really doing on the fifth Britain, then?' said Jay. 'Were he and his entourage really looking for a new home? Were they exiles?'

'That is unknown. The books we have were written before that occurred, of course. If any records were created afterwards, they are presumably on the fifth Britain.'

'Is that where we are going, then?' I said.

'It is. The scroll-case and its map suggest that Torvaston had a mission planned in advance of the disaster at Farringale. I want the two of you to find out what it was, and what became of it.'

Jay and I were silent for a moment, figuring out everything Milady had not specifically said.

'The maps were of the fifth Britain, were they?' I said. 'The Vales of Wonder, and the Something Mountains?'

'Hyndorin,' supplied Jay.

'Right.'

'Since that is where Torvaston ended up, it seems likely,' said Milady. 'But there is nothing on the maps to confirm it beyond doubt.'

'And the books? Do they explain why he wanted to go to those two places?'

'Not in clear terms. However, the Court believes that the mission was bound up with the question of the sources of magick, and its connection with what are sometimes called the beasts of mythology.'

What had Torvaston's scholarly book been called? *A Treatise Upon Magicke: Its Sources and Histories*. Something like that. And we'd heard that the fifth Britain had a much more thriving population of creatures like griffins than we did. Coincidence? Perhaps not.

Furthermore, the griffins of the fifth collected in places like the very Vales of Wonder Torvaston had been heading for.

I had to agree with the Court: there was a clear case for investigation here.

'Is this a solo mission?' said Jay. 'Sounds like it's coming from the Court.'

'They have proposed a joint effort.'

'And you were saving us for this,' I said, rather cheekily.

'I was.' Milady admitted it with perfect serenity. 'The Court undertakes to spearhead this venture, at least officially.'

'So technically, we are working for them again.'

'Technically.'

'And the Ministry?'

'The Hidden Ministry will be informed once we have solid findings to share.'

I grinned. 'Top secret mission it is.'

Jay glanced at me. 'Who are they sending to go with us? I assume we'll have help.'

'That is not yet known. You have one day to prepare, and will depart for the Fifth tomorrow. Whoever is to accompany you will be here by then.'

I understood from Jay's sideways look that he was worried it might be Alban.

It probably would be Alban, to be sure. But was I worried about that, too?

I rather thought not.

Maybe?

No.

'Is there anything else?' I said, dismissing the subject from my mind.

'Yes. Don't forget to take the moonsilver lyre.'

'Ves shouldn't touch it,' Jay said quickly.

'Then you may carry it.'

He saluted. 'Yes, ma'am.'

'And, Ves, if you can contrive to take your unicorn companion along, you may also find that a useful measure.'

Who better to take on a find-the-mythological-creature game than a unicorn, indeed?

'I imagine it can be managed,' I said. 'Are we using Millie again?'

'The Court has prepared her for service.'

I hoped the process had proved a pleasant one for Millie, whatever it had entailed.

'There is one more thing,' said Milady, as I rose from my chair.

I paused. 'Oh?'

'If at all possible, I want you to find Miranda.'

I froze. 'What?'

'And take her with you.'

'But— but she's a traitor.' That was Jay, sounding unusually upset for him.

'She remains among the foremost experts on magickal beasts in Britain.'

'Are there more? Can't we get one of the others?'

'They are unavailable.'

'Why?'

'Two are somewhere in South America, in search of the camahueto. They have been gone for some months, and are not expected to return for some time. One is too elderly, at ninety-seven, to accompany you on any such venture. And the last placed himself beyond our reach when he accepted an offer of employment from Ancestria Magicka.'

Jay was frowning fiercely. '*Miranda* accepted an offer of employment from Ancestria Magicka, and betrayed us on her way out.'

'She may appreciate an opportunity to make amends.'

'Or she may betray us again.'

'Find her, please.' Milady's voice developed a rare note of steel. 'It is my belief that you will be glad of her expertise.'

'Yes, ma'am,' I said quickly, forestalling Jay's next objections with a slight shake of my head.

'Excellent. Good luck, then. Please report first to Orlando. He has some new equipment you may find useful.'

Jay and I trailed out.

'Well,' said Jay, with a frustrated sigh. 'Marching orders. Only: where do we even begin looking for Miranda?'

'Good question,' I said. 'But I have a feeling she never left the fifth Britain. And if she didn't, there's one person who might know where to find her now.'

Jay nodded. 'Right. Time to go see Zareen.'

Also By Charlotte E. English

Modern Magick

The Road to Farringale

Toil and Trouble

The Striding Spire

The Fifth Britain

Royalty and Ruin

Music and Misadventure

The Wonders of Vale

The Heart of Hyndorin